THE WICCAN'S HUNT

THE WICCAN SAGA
BOOK 2

AYLA VOLK

ISBN: 978-1-963113-04-4

PREFACE

The Wiccan's Hunt is the second book of The Wiccan Saga, a paranormal shifter romance series. For the best reading experience, it is recommended to read this series sequentially. Recommended reading age is 18+.

1

Juniper

My face peeked out from the icy cerulean blue waters, and I looked across the mirrored surface, reveling in the serenely quiet atmosphere. My legs slowly kept me afloat as I trod water in the middle of the lake that was surrounded only by the towering snow-covered mountains wrapped in a thick blanket of conifer trees. I turned my body, allowing it to float upon the stilled surface so that I could stare up at the clear blue sky. My arms skidded across the surface as I felt the pull of energy entering my body.

"Juniper," a deep, familiar voice called across the water.

I dropped my body back below the shelter of the water and turned to look at Forest, my mate, calling me from the rock-crested shoreline. I smiled at him and began to swim in his direction. The splashing of the water from each penetration of my arms and legs disturbed the peaceful quiet that I had been savoring, but with his appearance, I knew that my time hidden away at this sanctuary had come to an end. As I neared the shore, I cast a silent thankful message to the water for its retreat. My bare feet helped to steady me as I found my footing, lightly stepping over the icy stones into the plush white towel Forest held out for me.

"How many times do I have to ask you to bring someone with you if you come up to the lake?" he asked, slightly annoyed.

I lifted onto my toes and kissed him lightly on his stubbled cheek.

"That would defeat the purpose of coming out here," I said, smiling back at him.

"What would happen if a rogue found you alone so far away?"

"First off, I would hear someone coming long before they could get to me," I said as I began to walk back into the surrounding forest in search of the bag he must have brought with him.

I found it nearby, placed on a decaying, moss-covered fallen log.

"Secondly," I continued, "I stick to the middle of the lake. I can swim to the opposite shore if anyone comes."

He knew that this was a losing battle, but he never relented. He grumbled as he followed me over to the bag. I finished drying off and folded the towel, sliding it back into the small black duffle before returning to Forest, my smug smile never failing. He walked up to me and placed his rough, calloused hands on my bare hips.

"I will never stop worrying about you," he stated softly.

"And I know I will never stop worrying about you, but I watch you run off on patrol or perform your Alpha duties, but I trust you, as you should me. I would link you if I were ever concerned," I attempted to assure him while wishing he could see my side of the situation.

He let out a heavy sigh, "I know. I trust you; it's the rest of the world that I do not."

I kissed him again, feeling him tighten his grip on my skin as he gave in. As our lips parted, he leaned his forehead against mine.

"If we did not have things to do, I would take you right here. Watching you emerge with water dripping down your bare skin is driving me wild," he said in a husky voice.

I bit my lip as I felt a warmth course down my body.

"We shall make up for it later, then," I said in a sultry voice.

He grumbled his agreement.

"What do we have to do?" I asked, stepping back from him to curb my desire for him.

"Oakley found him. We have a phone call with him in an hour."

My muscles immediately tensed.

"We don't need to do this now if you want to wait," he added, sensing my demeanor change.

I took a deep breath and straightened my shoulders.

"No, I'm ready. I have spent my whole life wondering about him. It's time," I said confidently.

Forest gave me a deep, reassuring hug before stepping back and slipping his sweats off, sliding them into the bag with the towel. Without another word, we both shifted into our wolves, my petite red wolf contrasting with his towering black wolf. He leaned over and lifted the bag with his mouth, and we took off southward, back to our pack.

Thoughts of the man we were about to talk to filled my mind on the journey back. I had never thought I would find out who he was, as was typical for my upbringing in the Whisper Creek Coven. The women of my coven traveled into cities in search of prospective suitors to impregnate them, never seeing them again. As far as I knew, I would be the first witch since my family came to America over a century ago to meet her father. Six months ago, I found out that my father was, in fact, an Alpha, a message relaid to me from the goddess Selene herself. Forest and Oakley had been helping me track down who it could be since my arrival in the pack, and today was the day that I would finally find out who he was.

As we arrived back at the towering brick building that is our home, I shifted and grabbed the loose white cotton sundress that I had left on the nearby lounge chair. Forest did the same and slipped on the same sweats he had worn at the lake. We walked through the main entrance and found our way to Forest's office. Oakley joined us only moments later.

"How was the swim?" he asked with his usual cocky smile.

"It was good, thanks," I laughed back at him.

"Your disappearing acts are going to give our poor old Alpha here a heart attack one of these days."

"I don't disappear," I challenged lightheartedly.

"Oh please, you went to work in the greenhouse this morning, and when he went to pick you up for lunch, you were nowhere to be found. Do you know how complicated you make my day when my Alpha links me in a panic, and I have to search high and low for you?" Oakley chided.

"Well, I would tell him if he ever let me go alone."

"Hmm, I wonder why that is," he replied, implying heavily of the same reasoning Forest had told me each time I made my way out to the lake.

"Enough, you two," Forest interjected as he watched us from his desk, resting his chin on his fist.

Oakley, the Beta of our pack, and I had become close

over my time here at the West Moon Pack. He was like the brother I never had, always teasing and razzing me. It was as if he had challenged himself daily to see if he could get a rise out of me, yet my years with Meadow had trained me well for someone with his personality. I mockingly squished my face at him before turning back to Forest.

"Get on with it, Oakley," Forest shifted towards him.

"Alright, you two know how long I've been going through the old records, which, by the way, I think we need to digitize. I found the records of all meetings held around May 2000. There were two that happened during that month. The first was with the Burntwood Pack. Their meeting was on the first of the month, but they would have traveled from the north, not putting them in the states at all, let alone Mount Vernon."

"What about the other meeting?" I asked him.

"The Silver Ridge Pack. Their territory is in southwestern Colorado. That would put their route right through Mount Vernon."

"When was their meeting?" Forest asked him.

"May 14th is lining up pretty good as far as dates are concerned."

"What was their meeting about?"

"Alpha Caspian was a new Alpha and made the rounds to a few of the larger packs to establish relationships and solidify their treaties."

"Do we have a treaty with them?"

"Not an active one. As you know, there was the rogue epidemic in the late nineties and early two thousand. Many of the packs had treaties to provide support if needed. After the number of attacks lessened, many of those expired. Our pack has only kept up with the treaties with our neighboring packs, those in British Columbia and Washington," Oakley added the last part for my account.

I was still learning the politics of the pack. I had known that we had treaties with other packs as the Alpha from the Moon Fall Pack had visited around a month and a half ago to resign their contract with us, something done once a year. The North American packs were pretty dispersed. I learned of three in Washington state and several more in British Columbia. Most of the packs generally lived in Canada due to abundant land and space between human cities. Forest's office phone rang before we could get more details about the Silver Ridge Pack.

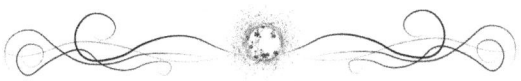

2

Juniper

We each stared at the phone momentarily, watching it ring.

"I'm going to set up a meeting for now. I feel like this type of news should be shared in person," Forest informed us before picking up the sleek black receiver.

"West Moon," he answered smoothly.

The heightened hearing from our wolves allowed both Oakley and myself to hear the voice on the other side of the line clearly. A gift that I had become incredibly thankful for over the last few months since my wolf finally emerged.

"Alpha Forest, this is Alpha Caspian. I received a message that you wanted to speak to me," a deep voice that held the weight of wisdom came through.

"Yes, thank you for returning my call. I would like to set up a meeting between us."

"What is this concerning?"

"It is of a sensitive nature, and I would like to discuss it in person."

"Hmm, I understand," he replied knowingly. "When would you like to have this meeting?"

"At your earliest convince."

"You are welcome to visit our pack next week."

"I know that it is customary for the requesting Alpha to visit the other Alpha's pack, but due to the *nature* of this topic, I believe it may be better for you to come to us."

"This is oddly suspicious, Alpha Forest. Perhaps if you could give me an idea of what this is concerning, it would help."

"You have a Luna, correct?"

"I do," Alpha Caspian's voice had a hint of warning.

"I believe it is something that you may not want your Luna to hear right away."

"I have no secrets from my Luna."

"I am sure, but this falls on a more personal matter."

The line was silent momentarily before Alpha Caspian responded, "I will come to you next Monday, but due to the questionable circumstances, I will be bringing my Beta and a group of warriors."

"Understood," Forest replied, "We will make the appropriate accommodations for your party."

They ended their conversation, and Forest placed the phone back on its base, looking up at me. I pinch my lip between my fingers as the uncertainty from the situation settled into my gut.

"Are you ready for this?" he asked me.

"I'll have to be," I replied nervously.

"Oakley," Forest turned his gaze to him. "Make the preparations. He didn't specify how many he would be bringing, but I can only assume by his demeanor that it would be more than we have room for in the pack house."

We had three guest apartments and three more guest rooms at the pack house to accommodate any visitors we may receive. I had only been in them a few times before. They were designed to fit seven couples, plenty if you asked me. At the coven, we never received visitors, so there were no spare beds at all. When Forest and I visited in the past, we stayed in my old bedroom, squeezing into the same small bed I had had since childhood.

"I'll help you, Oakley," I offered.

I could tell that it would be a good deal of work in a short amount of time. This was for me, so I felt I should take the lead. It would also help keep me busy so I didn't lose my mind from worrying before the meeting with my possible father.

"It's settled then. We have three days to prepare," Forest said as he leaned back in his chair.

Oakley and I left Forest's office, and he led me directly into his own. He walked around his sleek wooden desk, plopping into a red leather chair.

"Let's get things ready for dear old dad, shall we?" He said in a humorous tone but with a heavy meaning underneath.

"Let's," I added, sitting across from him.

We reviewed what needed to be done in each room and food preparations. A certain formality was expected when other Alphas visited—formal meals, a tour of the town, accommodating whomever he would bring. The complexity of it sent my mind whirling. I jotted down a list of tasks to accomplish before standing, determined to complete it. As if he had been listening for our conversation to finish, Forest leaned on the door frame to Oakley's office.

"Shall we have dinner?" he asked.

"Yes," I confirmed with a stiff nod of my head.

I was famished. I had skipped lunch and instead headed straight to the lake after my time in the greenhouse. Forest smirked at me and reached out his hand, offering it to my own. I laced my fingers through his as we walked through the back hallway to the kitchen. Our head chef, Joan, was stirring a pot of what smelled like delicious tomato and basil bisque.

"Alpha, Luna," she bowed her head to us. "Are you ready for your dinner?"

"We are," I said, licking my lips.

She smiled at me and gestured to the dining room.

"Don't forget about us," Oakley chimed in from the back hallway where we had just come in.

August was a step behind him as they came into the kitchen. We all went to the large dining room and took our seats. Forest sat at the head of the table while I sat to his left. Joan quickly made her way out and walked around the table, filling our waters. She made it seem so formal every time we sat down for a meal, another reason I typically avoided the dining room and would instead steal a plate to eat at the counter in the kitchen. As she returned with a beer for each of us, I could see the look of accomplishment on her face for getting us to sit and be served, as she felt it was fitting for the Alpha and Luna. I could only smile at her as she returned to the kitchen.

"What do we know of the Silver Ridge Pack?" Forest asked August, his Gamma.

"They are located in southwestern Colorado. They have around five thousand acres of private land surrounded by national forests. They run a cattle business called the Silver Ridge Ranch. They had around one hundred pack members from our last record with them. That was back in 2004, so I would assume that it may have grown slightly since then. They were known to be a powerful yet peaceful pack. They had their share of problems with the rogues back in the day, so they sought us out for a treaty. We kept the treaty up for five years before letting it fall to the wayside as there was no longer a need to keep up with it."

Forest nodded and looked at Oakley as Joan brought a tray of soups to serve us.

"What have you worked out so far for accommodations?" Forest asked further.

"We will put Alpha Caspian, his Beta and highest-rank warrior, in the pack house. We will prepare the other rooms if he chooses to use them for his additional warriors. The remaining warriors, however many there may be, will be housed in one of the tents. We will set up twenty beds in there. Hopefully, they don't bring an army. Otherwise, I will run out of room for them."

"I think twenty beds is plenty. If they bring more, we will make do," Forest responded.

After reviewing a few more details of the upcoming visit, we finally sat back and enjoyed the rest of dinner. Joan had made us a delectable meal of roasted herb chicken with rice pilaf and steamed asparagus. Ever since I had gained my wolf, my appetite had grown substantially. I now ate almost twice as much as I had when I first arrived. My snacking had also increased, though I still preferred the taste of vegetables and proteins compared to the processed food some of the others indulged in.

After dinner I headed up to our apartment to call my Gran. We talked on the phone fairly regularly. They had kept my place in the coven, which made me feel like I was a part of it. We tried to visit once every other month to see them. I picked up the cell phone Forest had given me. Gran and the others at the coven were the only other people I talked to, so I had never gained the habit of carrying it with me. Instead, I kept it plugged in at a small desk in the apartment. I clicked on my Gran's contact and listened as it began ringing.

"Hello," Violet's familiar commanding voice answered.

Violet was Gran's sister and one of the elders of our coven. Being the oldest, she was the leader of the group. Age declared your role within the settlement I had grown up in.

"Hi, Aunt Violet, it's Juniper. Is my Gran around?"

"She is. I'll get her for you."

"Thanks," I said as I heard her call away from the phone.

My Gran picked up a moment later, "Juniper, I'm glad to hear from you. How are things?"

I sighed before answering, "Oh, a bit complicated at the moment."

"What's going on?" she asked in her calming voice.

"We are pretty sure we figured out who my father is, and...he's coming to visit on Monday."

The phone went silent for a moment.

"Gran?" I asked, checking to see if the call had dropped.

"Are you sure you want to meet him?" Her voice was near a whisper.

"No, I'm not sure," I confessed. "But packs are all about family and connections. I discovered that I have this whole other side to me. Even though Forest has helped me understand what it means to be a shifter, I want to know more about my origins."

I wanted to know who he was. Watching the families around the pack made me question if I had a bigger family somewhere. Brothers, sisters... I had the opportunity to find out. And if I were ever to meet them, then perhaps I could be myself, my true self, around them. My mother died trying to give me a sister. What if I had one out there? There are too many questions that I have for me not to go through with this.

"I think you answered your own question. If you feel like you need to know more, the best thing to do is find out. I can't say that I understand your reasoning, but I respect it."

"Thank you, Gran," I told her, relieved.

"You're welcome, my sweet girl."

I heard a rustling through the phone when another familiar voice screeched through, "Juniper! When are you coming down to visit us again? I miss you."

"Hey, Meadow. I don't know when. We have some stuff going on up here, but I promise I'll let you know as soon as I get it sorted."

"Well, when you do, make sure to bring that sweet thing with you."

"You mean Forest?" I laughed.

"Um, yes! He's fun to look at. Besides, maybe we can rope him into doing some of these heavy chores my ma keeps putting on me."

"Oh, I see your real reason."

"Well, you know, someone had to run off with her wolf man and live a life of luxury while the rest of us are still being driven into the ground washing dish after dish!"

"Your mom still has you on dishwasher duty?"

"Yes, and I don't have you to help me anymore, remember?"

I laughed again, "I do, but I have faith in you."

"Sure, sure. Anyway, tell me about all the amazing adventures you've been going on?"

"I don't really go on adventures here. I've told you that. Life in the pack is very similar to life at the settlement. We have our jobs and our town; we have some gatherings, though nothing like back at the coven," I teased. "Although still plenty of naked bodies running around, just not in the fun way like we do."

"Well, you can't beat dancing naked under the full moon. Do you guys think you will come down for another one at some point?"

"Full moons are hard to do."

"You were able to make it down for that one a couple of months ago."

"You mean when I needed the coven to help me shift?"

"Yeah..."

"Special circumstance. The pack does their own full moon celebrations anyway."

"Do you get to dance naked," she quipped.

"Not much. I try to get out to do it on my own, but you're right. Maybe I should come down soon and join you."

"That's what I'm talking about!" she yelled excitedly.

I could hear Forest come in. He had stopped at his office after dinner to finish some things up. I looked up at him and smiled.

"I need to get going, but tell Gran I love her, and I will call again in a few days."

"Will do! Ciao ciao for now."

"Bye, Meadow."

I chuckled as I returned the phone to the desk and joined Forest on the sofa, curling myself under his arm.

"How are you doing?" he asked me.

"I'm fine, just a bit nervous. I mean, my mom did kind of trick him into impregnating her. Do you think he will be angry?"

"He might, but I don't think it would be directed at you. You're his daughter."

I pursed my lips, still not convinced.

Forest continued, "If he does, then you will know what type of man he is. There was more than one reason I wanted this meeting to be held here rather than at their pack."

I looked up at him, surprised.

"He would control the situation if he were on his territory. If he were angry, defending you against his whole pack would be hard. Here, every one of our pack members would defend you."

"I hope it doesn't come to that," I replied, a newfound fear settling into my stomach.

I had not accounted for the wrath an Alpha could bestow when angered. I had never personally seen it but had been taught of some historical instances. I recalled one story where an Alpha was insulted by a visiting pack and ended up slaughtering all of them. It caused a war between the two packs and their allies, lasting nearly five years.

"I did not tell you that so that you would be scared," Forrest pulled me from my thoughts, "I wanted to let you know that I have thought of every situation. I would be surprised if it went there."

"Okay," I said, still not wholly convinced.

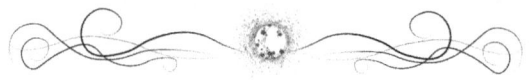

3

Juniper

The following day, after working in the greenhouse, I headed back to the house to start preparing for the Silver Ridge visit. I sat down with Joan to work out the meals that would be served.

"We will plan for three days just to be sure," I told her. "Let's plan for twelve settings all together. Once we see how many people actually arrive, we can figure out how to feed any others. I will talk to the crew down at the diner and see if they can accommodate any extras for meals; otherwise, perhaps we can deliver some food to their tent."

"Yes, Luna," she replied, jotting it down on her notepad.

"I think we should get a few more hands in here to help you out."

"I can ask Willow and Rowan," she offered.

They were the housekeepers in the pack house and were familiar with how things ran here. They would be a good choice, but it could affect their already heavy workload from having visitors.

"I think we need to look outside of the pack house. They will have at least three more apartments to keep up with each day. I was planning on looking for an extra set of hands for them, too."

"Aster and Glenn have helped out in the past," she added.

"Great idea! I'll stop by their places later today and see if they are available."

I jotted down a note for myself to remember.

"What would you like to serve?" she asked me.

"I trust you to come up with that. You are an amazing chef," I boasted about her.

"Oh," she said bashfully, "thank you, Luna. I will do my best."

"I know you will," I smiled back at her.

After sitting down with Joan, I informed Willow and Rowan of what needed to be done. Willow said her sister Holly should also be able to help us out. I was thankful for her suggestion, as it took finding someone for the task off of my list. As I trotted down the stairs, Forest emerged from his office, meeting me at the bottom step.

"Where are you off to?" He asked with a smile at the corner of his mouth as he watched me with amusement.

"Heading to the diner, Do you care to join?"

"Sounds good. Should we let Joan know?"

"Already done," I said, grabbing his hand and pulling him towards the door.

We grabbed our jackets and headed out, walking down the drive and into town. This time of year, the sun sets early in the day. Even though we were going for an early dinner, night had already covered the earth with its cool embrace. The light reflected off the roads from the street-lights overhead. I could see clearly into each of the shops along the street, which were just preparing to close for the day.

The diner was one of the hot spots for our community. Many people either gathered here or at the bar after their day. Forest had been hesitant to allow a bar to open. Even though wolves had an extremely high tolerance for alcohol, they could still overdo it, and with our naturally aggressive nature, it could easily lead to bad situations. The recent addition to our town was only opened after they agreed on a ten-drink maximum per person, the equivalent of two drinks for a human. It was more of a social setting, a place for people to gather outside of the crowded diner or cafe. With nearing nine hundred pack members, we needed to grow with our population.

We walked into the fifties-styled diner and found Rose darting from one table to another, her arms loaded with plates. When she spotted us, she quickly made her way to the hostess stand.

"Alpha, Luna," she said, bowing her head to us. "I have a table just about to open up."

"No rush, Rose. We can wait," I smiled at her. "Do you have a quick moment to talk with me?"

She set the menus that she had gathered down to give us her full attention.

"Of course, Luna. What can I do for you?"

"We will have another pack visiting us next week. We are unsure how many they will be bringing. Can you plan to fit them in for dinner, if necessary?"

"Absolutely, Luna. I can set aside a few tables for them."

"That would be great. Thank you. You can charge us for their meals."

We had an economy within our pack. Nothing was free, but no one went without. It was a way to support those around us. We each needed things that the pack could not provide, such as furniture, televisions, computers, those types of things. Houses were provided to everyone, and there were a number of cars that people could borrow if they needed to get around outside of the pack. Since we already had a functioning town, we charged as one normally would. If someone did not have enough money for what they needed, the establishment would serve them anyway and send the pack the bill. The debt would be paid back through some sort of labor or service to the pack. It made it so that everyone was taken care of comfortably, and no one had to worry.

A table near one of the windows opened up, and Rose hurried over to clean it before seating us.

"Do you two need menus tonight?"

"No, thank you," I replied. "I'll just have a burger with a side salad."

"And for you, Alpha?"

"The usual," he replied in a relaxed tone.

"I'll have it right out for you."

She dropped off our drinks, already knowing what each of us wanted. The familiarity came with the small town. Everyone already knew everyone and what they liked.

"It sure is busy for being so early," I told Forest looking at the packed diner.

"It's winter. Jobs are letting out early."

"That makes sense. Hey, I had a thought, and I wanted to run it by you," I told him as he leaned forward.

He cocked an eyebrow at me but gestured for me to continue.

"I was thinking that maybe I could go down to my coven to celebrate with them on the next full moon."

"You know that it is hard to get away for the full moon,"

he answered. "I need to lead the pack on our run. With winter upon us, I want to be there just in case there is a problem. Perhaps we can go when it warms up. Maybe April or May?" he offered.

I pursed my lips at the thought of waiting so long. Ever since Meadow had made the suggestion last night, the thought of it built up inside of me. The prospect of celebrating the full moon and harnessing Selene's power along with my coven was something I longed for. Here, though I ran with the pack and was out under the full moon, the blessing that the coven asked of Selene was more powerful. I had felt like my powers had weakened slightly without it. I tried the last full moon to do it by myself, but it was not the same. We were stronger when we were together as a coven.

"It will come faster than you know," Forest tried to comfort me, sensing my disappointment.

"I really think I need to go. I can feel the drain without it," I pushed.

He sat more upright, leaning closer to me, "What do you mean?"

"It's becoming harder for me to cast a spell. It's like running on a half tank of gas all of the time. I have it, but it's not nearly as powerful."

He leaned back and ran his hand through his thick hair, "Let me think on it for a while."

"Just promise me you will," I pleaded.

"I will," he answered thoughtfully.

4

Juniper

The next few days flew by faster than I had hoped for. Even though I had tried to keep my mind at ease from all of the 'what-ifs,' they still plagued me when I allowed my thoughts to wander. We had received word that the Silver Ridge Pack would arrive late in the morning. I paced back and forth in our bedroom, staring at the pile of clothes on the bed. Forest came in from the hall and watched me momentarily before approaching, wrapping his strong arms around my waist.

"It will be fine, Juniper. You need to stop overthinking it."

"I am meeting my father for the very first time. I don't think I'm overthinking anything," I argued back.

He quickly breathed through his nose, showing he knew nothing was getting through to me.

He looked down at the bed, "what's with all the clothes?"

"I don't know what to wear," I said frantically.

He laughed deeply before guiding me over to the edge of the bed and sitting me down.

"You look beautiful in everything you wear," he said softly as he tucked a stray hair behind my ear.

"Forest, this is my first time meeting my father," I pouted.

He chuckled, "Yes, you've already told me."

He looked across the pile, grabbed a turmeric-colored maxi dress with a smocked waistline, and passed it to me.

"You should wear this," he stated.

"Why this one?" I asked, looking at it.

"It looks good on you. I think it shows your personality, your love for nature, yet it still looks refined."

I let a breath go that I hadn't realized that I had been holding. He was right. This dress expressed all of those things.

"Thank you," I whispered out.

"You can thank me by letting me help you get dressed."

"And why would I do that?" I asked before biting my lip.

I already knew what he wanted. He pulled me to my feet and lifted my satin pajamas inch by inch up my stomach.

"Because I want to see what's underneath this," he said as he leaned towards my neck, kissing my bare shoulder.

I let out a small moan as I felt his hot breath skate across my skin.

"I..." I began to protest, thinking it was not the time, but my need for him swelled within me like a seedling taking root.

"Forest..." I moaned out.

It was all he needed before he lifted my shirt over my head and began sucking on my skin, his tongue sweeping up to my chin. I wrapped my arms around his neck, angling my head back to give him better access. I closed my eyes and rolled my head, savoring the sparks and heat already traveling my body. His hands, which had found their way back to my waist, moved downward, hooking a finger at the top of my sleeping shorts and pushing them down. They dropped to my feet, displaying my bare body to him. I could feel him harden within his pants as it pushed against my stomach.

When his head pulled back, our mouths crashed together. Our tongues twisted and danced with each other as if they were in their own love affair. I grabbed the hem of his grey t-shirt and desperately pulled it upwards. We both took in a breath as our lips parted, allowing him to free his chiseled chest from its confines. Our eyes were locked, the desire evident in each. He unbuckled his belt and slid down his jeans before kicking them off.

We stood before each other in our bare state, appreciating one another. He moved his hands down my body until he hooked the top of my thighs and lifted me onto him. My legs wrapped around him as our lips came back together. He moved us onto the messy bed, laying me on the heaps of scattered clothing before kissing down my body. He traveled farther and farther south until I felt his tongue run between my folds. My thighs wrapped around his head, and my fingers tangled in his short, messy black hair.

I moaned as his tongue entered me, rolling around before returning to my clit. It swirled around it repeatedly as his hand moved, and he slipped a finger inside. He continued to work me over until I teetered on the verge of an orgasm. He slipped in another finger, pushing me over the edge, and I succumbed to his efforts, throwing my head back onto the bed as my body tightened. He licked up my juices before climbing back over me, aligning himself.

With one confident thrust, he entered me to his hilt. A gasp left me as I adjusted to his size. He leaned down and kissed me deeply as he began to move himself. Tasting myself in his mouth only ignited my lust further. My legs were wrapped around his waist, and he gripped my underside, bracing me for him as he pushed into me again and again. I could feel his manhood slam into the back of me as I reveled in my own pleasure. He was quick to make me come again before I forced us to roll, landing me on top.

Straddling him, I leaned back, rocking myself while I felt every part of his length rub against me. I moved quicker, matching the growing sensation within me. I lifted my body and slammed back down on him again until my body exploded in ecstasy once more. At the same time, I could feel him swell, and I watched as his face pinched together as he released himself, filling me. I rode him out until I could tell I had taken every drop from him. Only then did I lean down and kiss him. I rested my head against his hard chest and listened to the steady beat of his heart and the air passing through his lungs. We lay like that for a while, taking a moment before returning to the chaos that the day was sure to bring us.

We slipped into the bathroom, grabbing a quick shower before dressing or redressing in his case. I sat down at the vanity and fixed my curly red hair, using a defuser to help it dry in time. Next, I sorted the clothes on the bed, tossing most into the laundry hamper and hanging those not dirtied from our escapade.

Forest came to the closet door, "They're here."

I tightened my fists at my sides as I nodded at him. He held my hand as we made our way down to the entrance, which was customary for welcoming traveling alphas. It reminded me of the old historical shows I've watched where everyone stands out front waiting for the carriage to arrive. Except in this case, the carriage was three black Escalades with blacked-out window tinting. The gravel crunched under the weight of their tires as they stopped in front of the pack house. I watched as men began to unload one after the other. I had assumed there would have been a few empty seats as shifters tended to be larger, but that did not seem to be the case.

When an older man who looked in his early fifties stepped around from the driver's side of the first car, I already knew who he was. His deep green eyes mirrored my own. The other new arrivals watched as he approached us, extending his hand to Forest.

"Alpha Forest," he greeted in his deep baritone voice.

"Alpha Caspian," Forest returned as he shook his hand. "This is my Luna, Juniper; my Beta, Oakley; and my Gamma, August. Thank you for coming."

"Luna," he greeted me with a slow nod.

I could feel the power radiating off of him, the same power I felt from Forest. He had explained to me that it was the Alpha aura. All high-ranking wolves had it, but you could never miss the heavy power that rolled off an alpha like a weighted blanket.

"Have we met before? You seem familiar," he asked me.

If only he knew...

"No, I do not believe we have."

He nodded before looking back at Forest. "I would like to know what issue needs to be divulged away from my pack."

"We can speak in my office," Forest gestured towards the house.

Alpha Caspian nodded again, and Forest led us into the house, heading back to his office. Forest held the door open for us, closing it behind us once we entered. Alpha Caspian took a seat on the sofa against the side wall. I followed his lead and sat in one of the chairs perpendicular to it.

"Can I get you a drink?" Forest offered.

"No, let's get on with it."

Forest sat in the chair next to me. He rested his hand on my knee, giving me the unspoken comfort and confidence I needed.

"Alpha Caspian, when you traveled here in 2000, did you stop in Bellingham?"

"What are you talking about?"

"I'm just asking a question if what I believe even pertains to you."

"I don't know where Bellingham is. We stopped at a few towns along the way," he hesitantly answered.

I could tell he was uncomfortable, which I understood, but I trusted Forest's approach.

"Bellingham is a small city in north Washington."

"I don't remember the town's name, but we stopped in northern Washington. Are you going to tell me what this is about?" He asked, obviously getting aggravated by the questioning.

"I will get to the point. Could you please bear with me for a few more questions?"

"Very well, but make it quick," he replied, his annoyance growing.

"I will. Did you stop at a bar while you were in this city?"

"Yeah, we had some drinks."

"Did you meet a woman there?"

Alpha Caspian's face had a mix of surprise and anger on it.

"Why do you need to know that?" he asked aggressively.

"Please just answer," Forest remained calm as he pushed further.

"I will not," he replied as his wolf's eyes flashed a warning.

"Then I will take it that you did. That woman was my mate's mother."

Surprised, he looked at me, "She was not a shifter."

"She wasn't," I smiled at him.

"How is this possible then? Are you a half-shifter?"

"I am," I answered honestly.

Realization and disbelief took hold of his face as he looked at me more intently, studying my features.

"Who is your father?"

"I, um, believe you are," I hesitantly told him.

His mouth dropped, and he stared at me, not making a sound. I began to twist my fingers together, waiting for his response. Clearly, he was in a state of shock, but how would he be once that wore off? Would he be willing to accept me? Would he storm out and refuse to acknowledge me? The weight of his silence weighed on me.

"Alpha Caspian," Forest called, breaking him from his trance.

He looked over at Forest and back at me a few times before regaining his composure.

"Why do you think that I am your father?"

"You were the only man my mother had ever been with, at least before she died."

"She died," he stated rather than asked. "My sympathies. She was a beautiful woman full of so much life. When did she pass?"

"She was raped and murdered when I was three."

Anger flashed across his face at my revelation.

"What happened to you? Did the pack find you?"

"No, my Gran raised me, along with my aunts."

"That must have been difficult."

"Only in the sense that I was missing my mother. I had a happy childhood full of love. Only when I was twelve did my Gran tell me what happened to her. It was hard to digest, but I worked through it with time."

"Whatever happened to the man that did that to her?"

"Honestly, I'm not sure. I was told he was caught, but I do not know what came of it."

His question reminded me of a comment from one of our weekly gatherings before I left the coven. Violet had mentioned that they had rid the world of the man who killed my mother, but I never had a chance to ask for more details. I would need to ask my Gran the next time I went home.

"He deserves only death. I only knew her for one night. When I awoke in the morning, she was gone. There was something about her that drew me to her. More so than anyone else I had encountered. I had even wondered if she were my mate by how strong the pull was. I stopped back at the bar on our return home, but she was nowhere to be found. I even asked around, but she had not been seen since the night we were together. The fact that she was human convinced me she would not have been my mate. I met my fated mate, June, a year later. I had always wondered why I felt such a strong connection to your mother, and now," he lifted his arm and gestured towards me, "I am even more perplexed."

Shifters, as I have come to understand, only mate with other shifters, at least for true mates. They can choose to mate a human, and there are such instances, but it is almost unheard of for them to produce a child. The fact that I was standing here, the product of a shifter and a non-shifter, would be a conundrum in anyone's mind.

"I can tell you are a wolf, though I sense you are different. How is it even possible that you are here? I have only seen two other records of half-shifters over the last two centuries."

"Honestly, I had no idea I was even a shifter until a few months ago."

"You didn't shift at sixteen?"

"No. It wasn't until after I mated to Forest that the change came on."

"I'm baffled," he confessed as he leaned back on the sofa with his hands behind his head, scratching at his scalp.

He ran his hands down his face before sitting back up and looking at me. "I can't believe I have a daughter," he said.

"Do you not have any others?"

"No daughters, but I do have three boys," the corner of his mouth tilted as he thought of them.

Brothers, I have brothers...

"What are their names?" I asked, desperate for more information.

"Jasper is my oldest. He is nineteen. Oliver is my middle boy. He's sixteen. And Cain, my youngest, just turned fourteen. And you are...twenty-two?"

"Yes, my birthday is February 15th."

He nodded appreciatively with a smile.

"Now I understand why you didn't want to discuss this in front of June. Hell, I don't even know how I will tell her, but I am sure she will love you."

Warmth spread through my chest at the feeling of his acceptance. I hoped that he would still feel the same if he found out about the other side of me, that I was a witch. I debated telling him right off the bat, but it had been so ingrained into me not to share my secret that I was more hesitant.

"How about we all join the others for lunch? We can discuss this more over the next few days."

We both agreed and stood, heading back out to join the others.

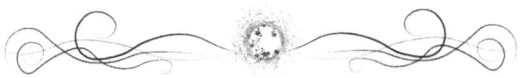

5

Juniper

L unch went smoothly and was followed by us giving the others a tour of the town. Afterward, we showed them to their rooms and the tent we had set up close to the training grounds. It was one of the only areas with enough open and leveled space to set it up. The rest of the town was thick with trees. The Silver Ridge Pack had decided to have the Alpha, his Beta, and lead warrior stay in the pack house with us while the other nineteen men would bunk in the tent. As they tossed their sacks on their beds, I ensured they had everything they needed before we returned to the pack house with Alpha Caspian and the others.

Joan had just finished dinner preparations, so we sat at the dining table almost immediately after arriving. Forest took his seat at the head of the table while Alpha Caspian sat opposite of him. His Beta, Leo, who was close in age to himself, sat to his left, and his lead warrior, Hank, sat to his right. Dressed in a tuxedo, Glenn served us as the waiter while Aster stayed in the back, helping Joan prepare the food.

"The chef has prepared grilled scallops with artichoke and a balsamic drizzle for your starter course," Glenn informed us as he began to serve the first course.

I didn't even know Joan could make food like this. After the first bite, I was instantly won over and decided to ask her to make it again.

"Thank you for your hospitality," Alpha Caspian said to Forest before he took his first bite.

"We are happy that you could make the journey."

"As am I," his eyes darted to me as he spoke.

As we ate, the dinner conversation was light. We talked about our towns a little more. I found out that they do things differently in theirs. They had a large pack house that the warriors and single people lived in. They also used it as their gathering hall and hosted all their events. The high-ranking shifters, such as Alpha Caspian and married couples and families, lived in their own homes. They did not have many businesses in their territory besides the cattle ranch and instead relied on the local town for most of their resources.

Beta Leo shifted the conversation back to us, "How long have you two been mated?"

"Six months now," Forest said, sending me a quick smile.

"Congratulations," he nodded his head at us.

"How did you meet? Based on your age, Luna, I assume you are not from around here."

I looked at him, trying to figure out what he meant.

"We met in the nearby forest," Forest interjected. "She was traveling close to our territory, and I caught her scent."

I didn't like the direction of this conversation. I was unsure how much Alpha Caspian had divulged to his Beta, and I did not want to cross any boundaries. It would be up to him to decide.

"Ah, yes," he smiled at us. "Nothing is better than that first whiff of your mate's scent."

"Very true," Forest agreed.

I was thankful when Glenn came in with the main course.

"For your main course, we have prepared a filet mignon with a mushroom wine sauce," he announced as he set the elegantly plated dishes in front of us.

This had become the fanciest meal I had ever had. I had come a long way from the hearty dishes I grew up with. I gawked at the delectable food before grabbing my fork and knife.

"So tell us of your birth pack, Luna," Beta Leo started again.

I froze mid-bite and looked over at him.

"She comes from a small pack, only, what? Ninety people?" Forest saved me.

"Oh, um, yes. There were just over ninety of us."

I noticed the suspicious look on Beta Leo's face, and the questioning look Alpha Caspian was glaring at him. From the question, I could tell he had not shared my heritage with him, so I was unsure how to handle the situation.

"How was it living in such a small pack?"

"I loved it," I smiled at him as I remembered the settlement. "I had a large family and was close to all of them. We spent most of our time in the forest or meadows when we were not busy with one of our tasks."

"Did you have much land?"

"We did, actually."

"Amazing. It's nice to see a small pack flourish."

"It is," I agreed with him.

We might not have been a pack per se, but we were something similar.

The remainder of dinner went more smoothly, lacking any hard questions. We finished our meal with banana fosters tiramisu and said our goodnights before retreating to our apartments. I had hoped to have more of a chance to speak to Alpha Caspian to learn more about my brothers, but I knew they must be tired after traveling so far, so I did not ask. Forest and I changed into more comfortable clothing and sat in our living room.

"How do you think tonight went?"

"I think it went well. Your father seems accepting of the whole situation."

"I agree, but he didn't seem like he wanted to share it with anyone else."

"Not yet. My best guess is that he will tell them tonight."

"You think so?"

"Probably, but we will watch what we say tomorrow, just in case."

I sighed and nodded.

"I can't believe I have brothers and three of them!"

Forest chuckled, "That's a lot of Alpha under one roof."

"What did you mean?"

"Alpha's produce alpha's. The fact that you were born a girl is a wonder all on its own. Alpha's typically produce a male heir, at least for their first. It is nature's way of ensuring the leadership of the pack."

"We only have girls in the coven. What does that mean for us?"

He looked at me solemnly, "I think we will just have to wait and see."

The topic of children had come up once or twice before, but it had turned into a sore subject. I had assumed that I would become pregnant quickly as we had never used protection. I always wanted children, as did Forest, but we had not been blessed by Selene yet. Hearing what Alpha Caspian had said tonight about the rarity of having a crossbreed made me question if it was even possible for us.

"Forest," I began to ask as I gazed at the wall, not able to look him in the eyes as I asked it, "what happens to the pack if I am unable to give you an heir?"

I could feel him looking at me.

"It would be passed to the next highest rank. Most likely Oakley's son."

I could tell the answer hurt him; I could feel it through the bond. I fought back a tear that threatened to spill out but took a quick breath in, letting it back out slowly.

"Shall we watch a movie?" I asked, desperate for a change of conversation.

"Sure, what would you like to watch?"

"Something funny."

I needed a distraction. The whole day had been a rollercoaster of emotions, and I was ready to turn my mind off and get lost in the screen in front of me. Forest grabbed the remote off the coffee table and switched on the television, scrolling through the list of movies until we settled on one.

6

Juniper

I must have fallen asleep on the sofa last night while watching the movie because I had no recollection of going to bed, yet there I was, cuddled up with Forest under the thick, warm comforter. I was not ready to wake up, so I lay there watching the sun rise through the window. I could hear the chirping of the birds outside, looking for any food they could unearth. A few tiny snowflakes drifted from the sea of grey that was cast over the top of us. Winter was here and it was gaining its strength each day. I was thankful for my newfound body heat, allowing me to wander into nature without much discomfort. I could hear Forest's breathing change as he awoke.

"Good morning, beautiful."

"Morning," I smiled at him before kissing his lips.

He rubbed my shoulder with his hand and seemed in no hurry to get up. I was grateful for the extra time before I had to face the rest of the world and all of the emotions the day would bring. The moment was fleeting, though, as he eventually kissed the top of my head and pulled himself up.

"Would you like to join me for a shower?"

I pulled the blanket higher, wishing it could shield me from the day, but I knew that this might be my last chance to learn more about my father, so I tossed it off of me and sat up.

"Sure," I forced a tight smile on my face.

Afterward, we walked down for breakfast, finding most of the others already seated at the table. They must have been early risers, like us.

"Good morning, Alpha Forest, Luna Juniper," Beta Leo said as we took our seats.

"Good morning," I smiled back at him.

Glenn came out of the kitchen and filled our glasses with orange juice and water.

"Will you be having coffee this morning, Alpha?"

"Yes, thank you, Glenn," Forest responded.

"And for you, Luna?"

"Tea, please. Joan knows how I like it."

He nodded his head and returned from where he came.

"I would like to meet with you both this morning if you have time?" Alpha Caspian asked from across the table.

"We can meet in my office after breakfast."

Alpha Caspian nodded and returned to the plate in front of him.

"Good morning to you all," Oakley said as he entered the room.

Even on his best behavior, Oakley's personality would shine through. He brought a wave of energy to the rest of us as we each returned his greeting. The casual yet restrained conversations that had been held at each meal so far felt awkward at best. It was as if each person could feel the tension floating overhead and were waiting for it to drop. As we finished eating, Forest pulled back my chair for me as we stood.

"Would you mind if my Beta joined us?" Alpha Caspian asked before we headed to the office.

Forest glanced at me for confirmation before replying, "Not at all."

The four of us entered the office, finding the same seats we had occupied yesterday. Beta Leo joined Alpha Caspian on the sofa.

"I have informed my Beta of your claim to be my daughter."

My claim? What does he mean, *my claim*? Does he not believe me? He didn't seem to doubt it yesterday. Surprised...yes, but excepting.

He continued, "While we can see similarities, I think you both can understand that there is some hesitance to accept it blindly. It would cause quite a stir within our pack for them to discover that an Alpha heir, a half-shifter at that, is, in fact, the Luna of the most powerful pack in North America. There may be questioning to the validity of it, and I would like to have concrete proof before I make an announcement."

I felt my heart racing in my chest. Was he trying not to claim me as his own at this point? It was a drastic switch of attitude since we talked yesterday.

"We have a doctor in town who can run the blood test, proving your paternity to Luna Juniper," Forest replied.

"We would like to use an outside source. You understand. We need to be sure that it is a neutral party."

"How would you like to proceed then?"

I could feel Forest's anger growing, yet he restrained it.

"Today, the four of us can drive to Vancouver and go to one of the human labs."

"We can do that, but my Gamma and lead warrior will join us. You understand, protection for the Luna," Forest said sharply.

"Then it's settled. We can leave now."

"I will gather my men, and we will meet you there. I will let you choose the lab. Please leave the name of it with my Gamma."

We all stood, and Forest and I watched as the others left. Forest walked over to the door and shut it behind them before returning to me. He already knew where my mind had gone.

"It's just a request, Juniper. I would ask the same if I were in his position."

"His whole demeanor has changed. He seemed casual yesterday, maybe even a little excited, and today, he is like talking to one of those lawyers we met with when I first visited Vancouver. It's all business."

"Alpha's are like that. There is a formality to it all."

"I understand that, but why the switch?"

"He was probably in shock yesterday and let his demeanor slip."

"I don't know Forest..."

He pulled me tight to his body in an act of comfort, which I happily accepted. He let me stay there until I was ready to pull myself together and go. I was surprised to see August and Cole, our lead warrior, already waiting outside of his office for us.

"Oakley is pulling a car up for us now," August informed us.

I quickly went to our apartment and grabbed anything I thought I might need, such as my ID and cell phone, before tossing it all in my cross-body bag and meeting the others at Forest's Range Rover. I climbed into the front passenger seat and buckled in. Forest took off slowly down the drive. He handed me a piece of paper as we hit the main road. I looked at the address written down on it.

"Can you type that into the GPS, please?"

I looked at the screen and felt intimidated. Despite my assimilation into the pack, I still had not used much technology. Besides the television and the occasional use of my phone, which Forest had programmed all the numbers into, I had steered clear of it. It wasn't that I didn't like it; I just had no use for it. I worked in the garden, and when I was not there, you could usually find me wandering around in the woods or watching a movie with Forest. Even when we had taken the car out to run errands, Forest knew where we were going. After I had not done what he said after a few moments, he glanced at me.

"Press the navigation button and then look for addresses and enter it in."

I smirked at him, "thanks."

We wove down the road, following the directions from the synthetic voice that continually barked at us. As we entered the city's outskirts, we found the place that Alpha Caspian had sent us to. It was a standard-painted concrete building with a large sign that read *DNA BC*. Inventive, I laughed internally. We climbed out of the car, finding Alpha Caspian and Beta Leo standing out front. The others waited outside while Forest, Caspian, and I entered the stale waiting room. There were only a few slightly worn chairs lining the sides with tables on either end scattered with old magazines and a counter where several women sat.

As we approached, Alpha Caspian began to talk to them, "Hi, I called ahead about a paternity test."

"Name?"

"Caspian Wilder."

It was the first time I had heard his last name. Surnames were not commonly used in the shifter communities. They all had them but everyone was addressed by their first name only. The woman began clipping papers to two sets of clipboards before passing them over.

"The father and child will need to fill these out. You can take a seat over there and bring them up when you're done."

Alpha Caspian nodded his head at her as he took the clipboards, passing one of them off to me. I had never had to fill out a form like this, but it was mostly self-explanatory. When we were finished, Forest stood and took both sets of papers, returning them to the woman at the desk before sitting back down next to me.

"She said it should only be a few minutes," he said to Caspian and me.

We waited silently until a woman in scrubs approached an opening at the side of the room.

"Juniper Nary," she called out.

I stood and followed her down the hall as she led me to a small examination room. The pale blue walls and absence of windows lacked any source of happiness. A counter was built into one wall with a plastic tote full of empty vials and a syringe on a napkin nearby. A chair was placed in the corner by the counter, and a small exam table was beside it, immediately to my right.

"Go ahead and take your jacket off and have a seat in the chair," she instructed.

I sat down, laying my jacket over my lap. Unsure if I was supposed to tell her anything, I continued my silence.

"Roll up your sleeve."

I grabbed the cuff of my green peasant top and tugged it

up to the top of my arm. She pulled a stool out from under the counter and sat on it. Reaching into the tote, she pulled out a small blue ball and handed it to me.

"Squeeze this," she montonely said.

It seemed like a strange request, but I did as she said. She wrapped a long rubber band around my bicep and laid my arm across the top of the counter. I watched as she picked up the needle and pointed the tip toward the protruding vein in my arm. My breath caught in my chest as it pushed into my skin. The only other time I had my blood drawn was when I was at the clinic my first night at the pack. I had been unconscious for it. I now understood the reason why so many people despised needles. She connected one of the vials to the end of the needle, and I watched in fascination as it quickly filled with my blood. She pulled the now full vial off the syringe, placing it on the counter before grabbing a cotton ball. She pushed it down onto where she had inserted the needle and pulled it out, holding the swap still as she dropped the needle into a red container connected to the wall and grabbed a piece of vibrant blue tape, wrapping it around my arm over the cotton.

"You're all done. It looks like you are doing the same-day results, so you should hear back by 5:00 pm tonight.

"Thank you," I replied.

We stood and left the room as quickly as we had come in. I pulled my sleeve down and made my way back out to Forest.

"How did it go?" He asked.

"I don't think I like needles much," I choked out as I held my arm across my chest.

He laughed at me and wrapped his arm over my shoulder, "no one does."

We waited outside for Alpha Caspian to finish. As he exited the building, he slid his jacket back on.

"We will see you back at your house."

I noted his lack of the word "pack." It was common among the shifter community to leave certain formalities out of conversation when in the human world. It was the only time you could address the high ranks without using their title, as we did not want to bring attention to who we were. We quickly loaded up and started on our return to wait for the results and discover what that would mean for Alpha Caspian and me.

7

Juniper

After we returned home, I went for a hike up to the lake. It was where I could find solitude and peace. My own little slice of heaven that I could retreat to. I loved being a part of the community, but sometimes, a girl just needed a little alone time. It was still in our territory but due to the rough climb to get to it, most of the pack members did not find their way there. I knew that my sudden departure right after our return would cause Forest to suspect where I had gone. I could sense him following me. He allowed me time to myself but would not let me wander away unprotected. I was grateful for that, though I still preferred to be completely on my own.

I pushed through the trees, revealing the smooth, glassy surface of the calm waters. Usually, I would shift and run up to the lake, but on this day, the air had become frigid, and I wanted something dry to change into afterward. I removed my heavy down jacket and hung it from a broken branch nearby. My clothes quickly followed, and I dipped my toes in the icy water. Goosebumps covered my skin as it reacted to the polar touch of the water. The easiest way to acclimate was to dive in. I did just that, making my way over the shallows until the bottom dropped out from under me, giving way to the depths that the lake offered. It took me only a few minutes to adjust. The lake felt no colder than the spring waters from back home, yet my body could handle it for much longer these days—a perk bestowed upon me by my wolf.

I slowly swam out towards the center of the silver-blue plane, savoring the solitude and detachment at the center. I dove down, immersing myself in the sheltered retreat beneath the surface. I continued swimming downwards, pushing myself as if the further down I swam, the more I rid myself of emotional turmoil. I was usually very level-headed, not allowing things to affect me so significantly. My father has turned out to be my Achilles heel. Whether it was my want to have an actual parent in my life, a sense of normalcy I had lacked as far as I could remember, or the feeling of rejection, I had not sorted out yet.

As my lungs began to burn, craving a heavy breath of oxygen, I turned upwards, kicking my way back towards the surface. The water around me lightened as the sun's rays penetrated its mass. I inhaled deeply as my head broke through, resupplying my body with its essential needs. I heard splashing to my left and looked over. Forest was swimming out at full speed, still fully clothed.

"What are you doing?" I yelled at him.

He stopped and looked up at me. His expression quickly changed from panic to anger.

"What were you doing?" he yelled back angrily. "I thought you were drowning!"

"I'm just swimming," I replied innocently.

He swam out to me at a slower, less frantic rate.

When he neared, he continued, "I felt your body suffocating."

I could hear the concern in his voice, though the anger still lased through it.

"I was fine. I just swam back up."

"Is this what you do up here? Nearly drown yourself?" He accused.

I was tired of his accusation, and my own anger swelled in me, "I don't nearly drown myself. You're overreacting."

"You were down there for over ten minutes. I could feel it, Juniper."

"I was in control," I argued back.

I never once felt panic. He should have felt that. People hold their breath when they swim all the time, pushing themselves. I could feel his anger and fear flowing through the bond. I took a deep breath, trying to be understanding. If the roles had been reversed, I would have also felt panicked.

"I'm sorry if I scared you, but I was safe. As soon as I felt myself running out of breath, I came back up," I tried to explain more softly.

"Ten minutes, Juniper," his angry voice morphing into exhaustion replied.

"That is pretty impressive," I smirked at him.

He grumbled at me.

"Come on, let's get you out of here," I said, looking over his clothing. He would have to shift when we returned to shore. Though our bodies ran warm, the constant freezing clothing would pull all his heat out, making him susceptible to hypothermia on the hike back. Together, we swam back to where I had entered the water. It was then that I noticed that he had not even removed his boots. They made a thick sloshing sound as he traversed the rocky shore, taking a seat on a fallen log. The only article of clothing he had managed to take off before diving into the lake was his coat, which would not make much of a difference with the rest of him drenched. While we could take the frigid temperatures, the wet clothing combined with the icy air and blowing wind would quickly suck every bit of heat out of his body. He might be able to make it without a problem, but shifting would be easier and more comfortable.

"Strip down," I told him.

I grabbed my clothing that was hung nearby and laid my shirt on the ground, placing my other things on top of it. I pulled the bottom two corners, along with the top two, tying them together with the sleeves. I grabbed Forest's coat and loaded his wet clothes inside, tying it together like I had done my own. Now, we could shift and carry our clothes back with us.

We both shifted, picked up our impromptu satchels, and started our journey back. The light dusting of snowflakes quickly thickened until an entire storm began to rage around us. A wall of white surrounded us on all sides. The ice-kissed wind whipped at our muzzles as we pushed on. Our wolves were made to handle this type of environment, though it slowed our travel. We could sense the pack's direction, ensuring we did not venture off course.

Stay close, Forest linked me.

Definitely, I responded as I pushed my body next to his.

We came upon the first houses on the outskirts of town, and I felt a sense of immediate relief. Though I never felt a sense of concern from Forest, I was still getting used to my new abilities, and the thought of being stranded in a swirling mass of snow still had roots within me. We shook the accumulated snow from our fur before shifting and entering the pack house. I slipped on a dress I had stored in the front closet, passing Forest a pair of sweats.

I had one goal in sight, and that was to head straight up to a steamy hot shower. That goal would have been fulfilled if Alpha Caspian had not stepped out of the dining room and stopped us.

"Juniper, I hope you can forgive my forwardness this morning."

My body tensed at his voice, and my tongue was caught; no words could leave it. I simply looked at him, unsure of where I stood on his attitude this morning. I felt Forest step up behind me, radiating his alpha presence.

With my lack of response, Alpha Caspian continued, "The call has come in. I am indeed your father."

I bit on the inside of my lip and tightened my fists before nodding curtly and resuming my initial path up the stairs, Forest right behind me. I stormed into our apartment, making my way directly to our bathroom. I ripped my dress over my head, tossed it on the floor, and started the shower. I turned the pressure as high as it would go and stepped in, feeling the burn of the heat. I leaned my head in the water, letting it run down my face. I felt Forest's calloused hands wrap around my waist from behind. He leaned down and kissed my shoulder, pulling me back into him. I turned around to face him, wiping the water from my eyes.

"I won't pretend to know what you are going through, but I know how strong you are. Even when Sienna was at her worst, you never let her get you down. Your father is just another person. He can only take as much as you are willing to give him."

I sighed and leaned against his chest. He was right. I was giving this situation with my father too much power over me, allowing him to hurt me when I had done nothing wrong. I needed to ground myself when it involved him. I had gone nearly twenty-three years without him and required nothing from him. Whether he accepted me or not was up to him. I did not have to worry about it.

We finished our shower and redressed. I took all the time I needed to fix my hair, not allowing myself to feel rushed. When we returned downstairs, it was time for dinner. The others, who had been waiting for us in one of the sitting rooms, joined us as we took our seats at the table.

As Glenn filled our drinks, Alpha Caspian stood, "If I may make an announcement before we begin?"

Forest nodded his head as all eyes were on the older Alpha.

"This visit of ours has been one of the most nerve-racking yet happiest I have ever traveled. I blindly trusted an alpha I had only heard of to come to his pack under mysterious reasoning. Upon my arrival, I discovered I had a daughter, and it was none other than this alpha's very own Luna! While I was caught off guard, the fact that I indeed have a daughter fills my heart."

He looked at me sincerely as he spoke. I could feel the hold he had on me beginning to surface once more. I knew then that he would either fill me with happiness or crush me.

He continued, "Going against the want to openly accept this wonderful woman as my own, my duty as an alpha had to come first. I needed to ensure that she was, in fact, my child. Even with my lack of trust, she did as I asked, and today, we confirmed that she is indeed my daughter, my eldest child. My only hope now is that she can forgive me for any ill tidings on my part as we navigated these uncharted waters. I will do whatever she needs for me to gain her trust."

The only surprised people at the table were each of our lead warriors, as they had been kept out of the loop on the reasoning for today's events. I had assumed that Cole had his suspicions after the trip to the lab.

"Thank you, Alpha Caspian; I look forward to getting to know you better," I replied.

"Please, call me Caspian, and when it suits you, you may call me Dad. We would like to stay a few more days if possible so that Juniper and I could get to know each other better."

I looked over at Forest, who was looking back at me. He was waiting for me to reply.

"I think that would be nice," I smiled back.

After two challenging days, I felt like I was getting what I had wanted from contacting him in the first place: a chance to get to know my dad.

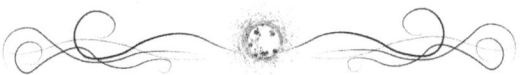

8

Juniper

The following morning, I invited Caspian up to our apartment so that we could find some privacy while we talked. I poured him a cup of tea as we sat on the large sectional sofa, sitting perpendicular to each other so that we could sit face to face as we talked. I held the steaming cup, breathing in the aromatic scent.

"My father was alpha before me. I was considered young when I took over after he was injured in the rogue war. I had thought that I had a few more years, but my father had lost the use of his arm. He could no longer lead the pack and passed it to me. I was fortunate that I had him to guide me as I filled my role. One of the first things I wanted to accomplish was to establish some treaties. I chose the five largest packs in North America and made my way to each one. That is how I met your mother."

I pulled my legs up on the couch and tucked them into my side. He was opening up to me and sharing his life story, one that involved me. I was hanging onto every word spoken.

"It was getting late that night, and we decided to pull into the next town so that we would arrive at the West Moon Pack at a good time the following day. A bar was across the street from the motel we had checked into. We decided to have a drink after having been in the car for such a substantial amount of time. As soon as I entered, your mother caught my eye. The way her red hair flowed down her back and the sound of her laugh was like a siren's call pulling me straight to her."

"I was smitten as soon as I approached her. No one could pull us apart that night. We eventually ended up back in my motel room. It was one of the most amazing nights of my life. I felt as if I was free from every obligation as long as I was hidden from the world with her...When I awoke the following morning, she was long gone. All she left me with was her name, Daphne. I've kept it hidden in my heart all these years, never speaking it again until today."

"You said you came back to look for her?" I asked as my breath held in my throat, hearing my parent's story.

"I did. I made sure we stayed there another day, staying in the same motel just for the chance that she would come back to look for me. I went to the bar again that night. When I didn't see her, I asked around. They all remembered her but told me she had only been around for the last week. I assumed that she may have been a traveler like me. In the morning, I checked all of the motels in the town, but no one had seen her. I realized that I had lost her. It broke my heart. Where did she go? I have always wondered."

"Oh, um," I cleared my throat, "she went home."

"Where was your home? You said you lived in Washington. Was it close to Mount Vernon?"

"I lived in a small town in north-central Washington, about an hour and a half away from Bellingham."

"What was it like? You shared a little about it the other night. I had hoped to hear more," he asked, his tone softer than his usual deep baritone.

"Well..." I bit my lip.

How much should I share with him? Was I ready to share that I was a witch? I needed to remember what I had decided on the night before. He could accept me or not.

"I grew up in a settlement, at least that's what we call it," I explained.

"Is that what you called the town?"

"No, the town was separate. The place I am from consists of multiple generations of six families. We call it the settlement because we settled on the land at the turn of the last century."

"Your family were pioneers?"

"Kind of...they left the old country, fleeing from violence, and went as far West as they could. The six families purchased the land with everything they had, and we are all still there today."

"That's fascinating," he replied, his eyes filled with curious wonder.

"Yeah, it is. I mean, it's what I grew up with, but I loved it. It was a very supportive community."

"Similar to a pack?" he questioned.

"Actually, yes," I beamed. The two were similar in many ways.

"So your home prepared you for living in the shifter world," he chuckled.

I returned his smile, "It did. It was easy, well, mostly easy coming in."

"What did you find difficult?"

"I didn't know I was a half-shifter yet. I guess I smelled human, and not everyone was excepting of a human Luna."

His expression turned serious, "I can only imagine. Shifters are protective of their own."

"They are, and it is something that I love about them. They are fiercely loyal."

I could see the pride on his face as I shared my views on shifters and their packs with him. I hesitated momentarily before continuing, having decided I wanted to share who I truly was with him. I could see now that he truly accepted me, and I needed to know if he would after he learned that my other half was a witch instead of a human.

"The settlement prepared me for more than just the community," I began slowly.

"How so?"

My eyes found his, relaying the seriousness of what I was to confess: "We lived in secret, too."

He looked puzzled, "I don't understand."

"Well," how should I put this? "See, I am not half human."

"But..." he looked at me as if he could uncover the truth. "What are you, then?"

"I'm actually half witch..."

His eyes grew as he looked at me with disbelief.

"You mean to tell me that Daphne was...a witch?" His voice displayed his disbelief.

"Yes," I confirmed. "The settlement is my coven."

He leaned against the back of the sofa and rubbed his hand down his face, scratching his short brown beard as he processed my new information. It was close to a full minute before he straightened up and looked back at me.

"I know very little of witches. There have been a few in

our vicinity, but I have never contacted them. They always seemed to keep to themselves."

"Yeah, we do that," I chuckled nervously.

"So, can you cast spells or something similar?"

I smiled at him, "I can. I'm an elemental witch, so I harness the moon's and nature's energy to give me power."

"I would have never known," he said, shell-shocked.

"Kind of the point. We stay pretty hidden."

He hummed in agreement, "Is that why your mother disappeared?"

"Yes," I replied hesitantly. This would be a difficult conversation for him, but honesty was always best. "Witches are only born female, so if one of us wants to become with child, we venture into the human world and look for a suitable...mate."

"So your mother meant to get pregnant with you?"

"Yeah. It's why she was in Bellingham. You must have happened at the bar she was looking in, and one thing led to another."

He cleared his throat before looking at me with a mix of sympathy and perhaps anger, "I...I don't know what to say."

"Usually, the father never finds out. It is why they leave the next day, to eliminate any chance of an attachment. If I had not discovered this other side of me, the one you gave me, I probably would have never sought you out."

"Why did you then?" He asked seriously.

I had thought about this at length. Why was it so important for me to find my father? It had never bothered me before finding out that he was a shifter.

"I was the only one to grow up without a mother. Once I discovered that you were a shifter and saw what that meant after having lived here for some time, I felt I needed to know

who you were. All I had to go on was that you were an
Alpha visiting the West Moon Pack."

"She knew what I was?"

"No, I figured that out later. No one in my coven knew."

"How did you find out about me then?"

The complicated topics kept coming up, sending my
mind into a frenzy.

"I'm not sure you would believe me," I answered softly.

His face softened, "I would like to try."

"As I said, not everyone was accepting when I first came
here. One of which was Forest's former...you know."

He nodded knowingly.

"Well, she may have kidnapped me from the pack house,
and well..." I said nervously, "stabbed me in the heart."

"She did what?" His anger swelled as he jumped from
the sofa.

His wolf's eyes came forward, and the veins in his neck
bulged. I reached up and held onto his wrist in an attempt
to calm him down. He looked down at me from my touch,
and I watched as his wolf slowly retreated.

Once I knew he had regained control, I continued, "She
lost her mind. She wanted to be Luna, and I guess she
figured that if she took me out of the picture, her wish
would be granted. Anyway, right before it happened, I was
transported somewhere, like in my mind. Selene talked to
me and told me that my father was an Alpha who had been
traveling to the West Moon Pack. She told me how to heal
myself. So once I came back to my body, I figured out what
her cryptic message meant, and I was saved," I shrugged my
shoulders, hoping that he would accept my explanation.

"What did Forest do during all of this?" He asked almost
accusingly.

"He lost his mind and scoured the entire mountain for

me. He found me. My Grandmother cast a spell, helping him strengthen our bond even more so that he could feel where I was, even though I was a long distance away," I explained with a smile.

"This seems like a story a mother would tell her pup rather than one of truth."

"Yup," I said, popping my 'P.'

"This is a lot of information," he said as he watched me.

"I know. If you want to take a break and, I don't know, digest all of it, I understand."

"No," he sighed, finally retaking his seat, "I only have so much time with you, and I want to make the best of it. You are my daughter no matter what."

His declaration that no matter what I threw at him, he still counted me as his daughter sent warmth through my chest. I could tell Forest could feel my happiness because it was paired with his own. We continued talking for the rest of the morning. It was like missing pages were being filled into my life's story—pages I had no idea were even missing. I felt my desire to know him being filled, and I knew I was coming to know myself a little better as well.

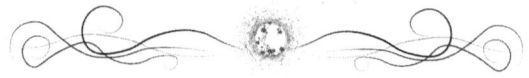

9

Forest

I sat in my office reviewing all of the patrol reports. It was not necessarily that anything of importance was brought to me directly; however, I liked to know what was going on to be sure that nothing slipped through the cracks. I was behind the last few days due to dealing with Juniper's father. Even if I had wanted to work on them, I would not have been able to focus due to the emotions she had been sending through the bond. It hadn't bothered me. Knowing she was in a difficult situation, I wanted to be there for her. Alpha Caspian's speech at last night's dinner was a welcomed turning point in their visit.

This morning, the two of them went up to our apartment to talk more. If he were not her father, my wolf would have been uneasy about her being alone in the room with an unknown shifter, especially a male, but I needed to allow her time to do this. I periodically took breaks from my work to focus on Juniper and see how it was going. I had already decided that if her emotion skyrocketed, I would go up, but besides the occasional slight nervousness, she was happy.

Join us for lunch, she linked me.

Be there in a minute.

I finished the report in my hand and filed it away before getting up and heading through the kitchen to the dining room. Everyone but Oakley, who had been out on patrol this morning, was already seated. They stood as I entered the room, returning to their seats after myself and Alpha Caspian. Glenn quickly filled my glass with water before disappearing back into the kitchen. He had done a fantastic job on this visit. I would need to give each of our pack members who had stepped up during the Silver Ridge visit a little extra for all their work. Their execution had been flawless, making me proud to present such a well-oiled pack.

The usual conversations began as Glenn returned with our first course, a beet and goat cheese salad. The uneasiness that had been lying beneath the surface before last night seemed lighter today, making everything more enjoyable.

"Alpha Forest, I was wondering if we could sit down after lunch to discuss some pack business?" asked Alpha Caspian.

I had expected him to ask at some point. Given our positions, some form of treaty would typically be in place.

"Yes, we can meet in my office."

He nodded his gratitude toward me, and the remainder of lunch went off without a hitch. Everyone seemed to be getting along well, and most importantly, Juniper was smiling. Alpha Caspian and I walked to my office, and he took his seat on the sofa.

I poured a glass of bourbon, "Care to join me?"

"That would be wonderful, thank you."

I poured a second glass and handed it to him before taking my seat. We each took a sip before we began.

"That's a good bourbon you have there."

"Thanks, it's Blanton's."

He nodded his head as he took another sip.

"I'm sure you know why I wanted to talk with you," he said.

"I have my suspicions."

"I'm sure you do. Now that we are connected through family, I want to discuss a treaty between our two packs."

"What are the terms you were hoping to lay out?"

"Standard fare...Our packs will remain at peace with each other. We will not aid other packs in acts of aggression toward our packs."

"So, just a peace treaty?"

"More or less."

"I think we can get that worked up before you leave."

August was our document writer and would have a template he could work off of.

I need you to draw up a standard peace treaty with the Silver Ridge Pack, I linked him quickly.

Yes, Alpha.

"I have another topic I would like to ask of you," his formal tone shifted lighter.

I leaned forward and gestured to him, "Go ahead."

"I would like to see if Juniper and yourself would travel to our lands. I want to show it to her."

"Why are you asking me instead of your daughter?"

"I know that she would need your approval to go. I would rather not ask if you were not comfortable with it."

I appreciated that sentiment. Juniper would be crushed

if I did not let her go, and before I could, I needed him to answer some questions.

"How do you think your pack will react to the news about her?"

"They will be accepting. They are good people," he assured me.

"And what about your Luna?"

Bringing in a child born before their mating could stir up trouble, and I would not risk it if there were even the slightest chance of harm to Juniper.

"I'm sure she will be surprised to find out and need some time to accept it, but I expect her to be welcoming."

"I will not bring her if she is to deal with a protective mate. She has already had her share of hard doings."

"Yes, she told me," he glared at me.

"She did?" I asked, somewhat surprised, ignoring his accusing stare.

"I cannot judge you for not waiting for your mate. Obviously, I did the same, but I wonder how the situation escalated the way it did?"

I would not take his criticalness to heart. She was his daughter even if they had just found each other, and shifters were just as territorial of their offspring as their mates.

"She clearly did not tell you the full story," I informed him.

"Care to fill in the blanks?" his tone was sharp.

"You may know the type," I began. "The she-wolf who has her eyes on the Luna position. From the start, I had made it clear that there would be nothing more than a little fun between us, but she tried to sneak past my boundaries. When Juniper arrived, she was livid and threatened her in our diner. I was prepared to put her to death, but Juniper asked for leniency. At her sentencing, she refused to accept her sentence, going on to threaten both of us. When I handed her a death sentence, her true mate, one I did not know she had, detonated an explosive behind the crowd. Her parents were in on the plan as well and struck the guards, incapacitating them long enough for them all to escape. While we hunted her down, she used the information she had gathered from her time in the pack house to slip past our patrols and take Juniper from our bed. She took her north, too far for our bond to reach. When I finally connected with her, we made our way to her and brought her home."

I intentionally left out any piece that would reveal Juniper's other half. She had not informed me if that had come up in their conversation earlier.

"Where are they now?" he asked with a danger in his voice.

"They were all executed."

"Even her parents?"

"Juniper had asked me to spare and exile them instead, but I would not risk them returning for revenge. We made it quick and out of the public eye."

His expression conveyed his approval of my information. "Does she know?"

"Yes. I don't keep anything from my mate, as we discussed."

He nodded in approval before taking another sip of his drink.

It had been a hard decision to make. They had only done what they thought they needed to save their child, but I decided that if they were willing to go to that length, I could not risk them returning. As Caspian finished his drink, he set the glass on the table.

"I will let you return to your work. We will be leaving

Friday morning. I need to return to my own pack," he informed me.

"I understand. I am glad that you could make it out."

"As am I, and I appreciate your discretion on the issue."

"Of course."

He stood up and gave me a quick nod before leaving. Things seemed to be falling into place for Juniper and her father. I was not entirely keen on her going to his pack yet. Their relationship was still developing, and I had no idea how his family would react, but if it were something that she wanted, then I would support her.

JUNIPER and I were settled into bed for the evening. The Silver Ridge Pack would be leaving tomorrow morning after breakfast. She had spent the last couple of days spending as much time as she could with her father, learning all about his life and family, and in turn, she had shared with him about her life back at the Whisper Creek Coven and of her time here with me. I had come to find out last night that she shared with him her heritage and her gifts. He had accepted her without hesitation and made me think highly of him.

Earlier this afternoon, we had sat down and finalized our peace treaty. Though it was standard practice when two high-ranking families came together, I could see what it meant for Juniper. It was another connection and statement of acceptance from her father.

"Did you know that all of their children go to public school?" She distracted me with another fact about the Silver Ridge Pack.

"It's not uncommon. Many packs rely on the local human towns to support them and their families."

"It's just so foreign to me. Even in the coven, we home-schooled. They taught us all the standard topics—math, science, you know—but they also taught us about our history and spells."

"Consider yourself lucky. Many shifter children have to hide that part of them in school on a daily basis."

"Do shifters ever go to college?"

"Sure. Some go to school in the city, and others take online classes. How do you think Dr. Stone became a doctor?"

"I had never thought about it," she laughed.

The way her smile lit the room made me smile in return. She had been like this for the last hour, constantly telling me more about her father's pack and asking more questions about our own. While I was happy she was learning more about shifters, I had only one thing on my mind, and I held it at bay for as long as I could. I leaned up on my elbow so I could better find her lips. She let out a small moan from my touch, making me instantly hard. The noises she made drove me wild. She gently held my cheek as she returned the kiss. I wrapped my arm over her waist, pulling her closer to me. As her body pushed into mine, the familiar sparks spread like explosive lava, driving my desire beyond what I could take. I pulled myself over her, deepening the kiss. My hand roamed upward, finding her breast, and kneaded it gently. I pinched her nipple between my fingers and slid my mouth down her neck, taking in every ounce of her alluring scent.

I could feel her own lust grow, matching my own as we became more fevered in our efforts. I slid my finger into her satin shorts and teased her clit a few times before sliding it into her. Her walls constricted around it as I pushed further in. I added another digit and rubbed her clit with my thumb to prime her for me. As I thrusted my hand back and forth, I took as much of her breast as I could into my mouth, devouring it. I could feel her tighten as I sent her over, my wolf preening in my mind as he did every time we satisfied our mate.

I pulled my sweats down, kicking them into our bedding, and pushed inside her. The same moan of excitement that she made every time I entered her was one of my top three favorite sounds. I moved in a steady rhythm, pulling back as far as I could without leaving this little piece of heaven before thrusting back in. Her heavy breaths were in my ear, and she gripped my shoulders. I could feel her building once more; she was close.

Alpha, we have a problem at the bar.

Fuck! I couldn't leave her on the cusp. I could take just another moment if it were at the bar. With one last strenuous movement inside her, she came undone, her walls tightening around me.

Alpha, I could hear Oakley call to me again.

I could barely give her time to come down off of her high before I kissed her and withdrew.

"I have to go. There's a problem."

"What?" She asked, frazzled. "What are you talking about?"

Her messy hair and her scattered thoughts made me want to climb back onto her and finish what I started even more, but it would have to wait.

"Problem at the bar," I told her as I tossed on a shirt and my pants.

10

Forest

I took off down the stairs, running as fast as possible to compensate for lost time. Watching her writhing in pleasure had made it had been worth it. I ran down the main street, and as I approached, I could see a crowd forming outside the bar.

"Alpha," several of my pack members called as I walked up. I held up my hand, needing to get to the root of the problem before I could begin my questioning. I worked my way through the crowd, finding my way inside. I had been hesitant to approve the bar. Drinking could lead to unsound actions like bar fights and drunken shenanigans. We had held a meeting to discuss it further, which the pack favored, opening an additional social space for them—one where they did not waste seating at the diner while others were waiting to eat. I had relented with the agreement of restrictions, yet here we were. I am here to deal with a problem only one month after opening.

I found Oakley and several warriors holding Clyde, the

bartender, and one of Alpha Caspian's warriors back from each other. Both bore the evidence of an altercation.

"What's going on here?" I demanded in my authoritative voice.

"These two thought that they would have a quick training session together right here in the bar," Oakley replied in his usual sarcastic tone.

"Take them both to the pack house and keep them separated."

"You got it, Alpha. Come on, boys. You're being sent to the principal's office," he said, dragging the warrior out the door.

"Let Alpha Caspian know of the situation," I called after them.

"You got it, Alpha."

After they were escorted out, I looked around at the crowd.

I told them, "If you saw what happened, stick around. Otherwise, the bar is closed."

While a few left, most stayed. This would be a long night. I returned to the small back office, found some paper and pens, and sat at the desk. As with all situations, I would need to interview all the witnesses. Cole knocked on the open door.

"Where do you need me, Alpha?"

I handed him the paper and pens I had collected, "Have each of the witnesses write out what they saw tonight and send them in one at a time for questioning."

"Yes, Alpha."

He disappeared back to the bar. I heard him call the first one back.

"Alpha," Savannah bowed her head to me.

"Take a seat," I gestured to the small folding chair across the desk.

She walked over, sat down, and looked up at me.

"Tell me what happened here tonight."

"I was sitting at the bar with Maisie and Sage. One of the visiting warriors was seated a few stools down from us. He had been there since before we arrived. We heard him yell at Clyde, wanting another drink. Clyde had cut him off. They began to argue when the warrior leaned over the bar and pushed Clyde back, knocking over several bottles. They all crashed onto the floor. Clyde came back and swung, hitting the warrior right in the face. The warrior pulled him over the top of the bar, and they began to fight, crashing into the tables. It was chaos!"

"So, from my understanding, you are implying that the visiting warrior started the altercation?"

"Yes, Alpha," she confirmed.

"Thank you, Savannah. Have you written down your account yet?"

"No, Alpha."

"Get a piece of paper and pen from Cole and fill it out. Once you're done, you may leave."

"Yes, Alpha."

Before the next person was sent in, Alpha Caspian came to the door.

"I heard there was a problem here tonight."

"There was an altercation between our pack members. Since one of them is your warrior, would you like to participate in the questioning?"

"I would," he replied, stepping into the room, grabbing the folding chair, and moving it to the corner.

And so we sat for the next hour questioning each of the witnesses. After we finished with the witnesses, Alpha

Caspian and I made our way to the pack house to question Clyde and his warrior. We moved to my office and called in Clyde first. He sat in the chair across from my desk.

"Tell us what happened tonight, Clyde."

"The visiting warrior came in around eight tonight. He took a seat at the bar and was having whiskey sours. He sat on his own all night, never conversing with any others. When he ordered another, I told him I could not serve him anymore as we had a ten-drink limit. He accused me of thinking he was drunk. I pointed to the sign on the wall, backing up the limited number. He claimed that he only had seven and could have three more then. I told him I rang up each drink under his tab and was certain he had ten. He continued to yell at me until he leaned over and shoved me into the bar. It knocked over several bottles, and some broke on the floor. I was angry and swung at him. After that, he pulled me across the bar, and we fought until Beta Oakley and the other warriors pulled us apart."

"You are certain that he did have ten drinks?" Alpha Caspian asked.

"Absolutely. I ring them in on the computer every time. You can check his tab and the cameras."

Check the surveillance cameras. See how many drinks the warrior had, I instructed August.

Yes, Alpha. I'm on it.

"Wait outside," I instructed him.

"Yes, Alpha," he bowed his head as he left.

"I am having my Gamma verify with our security footage," I informed Alpha Caspian.

He nodded his head at me.

Bring in the warrior, I linked Oakley.

Only a moment later, Oakley opened the door, and the

warrior walked in. He stayed standing across from us. Oakley left and closed the door.

"Callan, what were you thinking?" Alpha Caspian asked, enraged.

"I apologize, Alpha. The man insulted me and tried to claim that I had more drinks than I had. He was ripping me off."

"He is claiming that you, in fact, had your ten-drink limit and has evidence to prove it." Caspian returned.

"He could have put those drinks in any time." he snarked, referring to the till. "I believe he wanted me out of the bar since I am an outsider."

Anger swelled inside of me from his accusation. My pack had been more than hospitable to these warriors, and I took his claim as an insult. We did not have many surveillance cameras around to limit the risk of any video being found of our kind, but I had insisted that they be installed at the bar in case a situation such as this came about.

"That is a strong accusation," I warned him.

"One that was earned," he argued back.

His argumentative behavior was considered an insult to my position and one I would not take lightly.

Alpha, I have the footage. He had ten drinks, August linked me.

Keep it up, I will be there in a minute to see it.

Yes, Alpha.

Oakley, I need you to watch the warrior.

Coming in now, Alpha.

"I believe we need to review the footage," I told Alpha Caspian.

At that moment, Oakley came in and stood behind Callan.

"Shall we?" I asked towards Alpha Caspian.

"Yes," he said, his voice laced with anger.

We walked over to August's office. He had the video pulled up on his computer. He played it quickly, slowing it each time Caspian's warrior was served a drink. It clearly showed the ten drinks he was served and the fight that followed after he requested another. August paused the video.

"I owe you an apology for the behavior of my warrior. As I do not want to risk our newly founded treaty, I will leave his punishment to your decision," Alpha Caspian said solemnly.

Typically, an Alpha would discipline his own in such a situation. Placing the decision on me put me in a difficult position.

"If he were one of mine, I would ask him to hard labor for one month for the altercation. However, lying to me and disrespecting another alpha would mean exile. If I felt that he disrespected me as an alpha, he would be condemned to death," I looked at him intently. "I do not believe that I should be the one to determine his punishment. We have strict laws with harsh punishments here. Only his alpha can make that choice."

"I will take him with me tomorrow and have him stand trial back at our pack. I will ensure a just punishment."

I nodded at him and followed him out. He collected his warrior in my office and led him out of the pack house. I called Clyde back into my office. Oakley joined me, standing behind him as I retook my seat.

"Clyde, I understand that you were adhering to my rule and were put in a difficult position. While the warrior initiated the fight, and I will not have my people back down, the fact that you threw the first punch means you encouraged the altercation. Had you stood your ground and told him to leave, I would have found you not at fault. As the bartender and manager of the bar, you will need to learn to de-escalate situations so that altercations such as these do not happen. We are temperamental people, and our tempers are known to rise when we drink. If I let a fight slide without consequence, another will follow."

"Yes, Alpha," he replied with his head down.

"You will perform one month of community service."

"Yes, Alpha."

Community service would allow Clyde to work still and remain at home with his family, but he would also be tasked with fulfilling jobs around the pack without pay each day.

When I returned to my apartment around three in the morning, Juniper was fast asleep, so I climbed into bed and pulled her into my chest, quickly falling asleep beside her.

11

Juniper

I woke early, finding Forest still fast asleep next to me. As I often did, I lay there for a few minutes and admired his robust features. It took everything in me not to trace over him with my fingers, as I didn't want to wake him. It still seemed surreal that this god-like man was all mine.

With the room filled with early morning light, I knew I needed to get up. Hesitantly, I slipped out of bed and went to the shower. When I stepped back into the bedroom in my towel, Forest was waking, stretching his arms out.

"You should have woke me. I would have joined you," he said with a groggy but mischievous grin.

"I figured you needed the sleep," I smiled back as I walked around the bed to him.

He sat up and turned so his massive legs hung off the side of the bed. I stepped between them and wrapped my arms around his neck, kissing him good morning. He ran his hands up the back of my legs, and I felt him tug the bottom of my towel, dropping it to the ground.

"I believe we left something unfinished last night," he said in a husky voice.

I smiled as I leaned into him, letting him take me.

∾

"So, what was the problem last night?" I asked as we walked downstairs for breakfast.

"There was an altercation between Clyde and one of the Silver Ridge Warriors at the bar."

"Is everyone alright?" I asked, concerned.

"They're fine," he assured me, but I decided to check in on Clyde later to be sure.

I had come to know most of the pack, and Clyde was one I regularly saw in town. His mate, Ginger, worked in the gardens with me in the summer and fall. She was kind-hearted, and when we were together, we often joked that our names should have been switched. Whereas I had long, curly red locks, she had deep brown hair reminiscent of a juniper's bark.

We were two of the first at the table, only beat by Cole and the Silver Ridge Lead Warrior, Brian. They were both chatting and sipping on their coffees. Upon our arrival, breakfast was served. Glenn brought out stacks of pancakes with bacon, roasted potatoes, and sliced fruit. Caspian joined us soon after, followed by the others.

"I would like to invite you two to our pack in the spring," Caspian spoke.

I was instantly excited at the prospect of seeing where my father lived. I looked over at Forest, unsure how he would feel.

Up to you, he linked me.

"That would be wonderful! Thank you for the invitation."

"You can meet your brothers."

"I look forward to it and to meeting Luna June."

"As I'm sure she will be to meet you," he smiled at me.

With one final goodbye, he turned and got into the driver's seat of his vehicle, waving as he and his entourage drove off. We stayed put, watching their cars disappear from view. It had been a nerve-racking visit but one I was thankful for. Caspian seemed like a nice man, and I looked forward to getting to know him better. It was still wild that I had a whole family out there. I wonder how many of my coven had the same. Most, I would assume.

Forest pulled me into his side and kissed my head, "I need to catch up on some work."

"Okay, I'm going to go check in on the greenhouse. Oliver has been covering for me this week, and I want to see if I can help."

We both went our separate ways. I walked through town on my way. It was still too early for the bar to be open, but I figured I would try my luck in case Clyde was in early. I looked in the front windows when I came to the painted brick building. I could see him behind the bar cleaning up. I knocked on the glass, grabbing his attention. He walked over and unlocked the door, holding it open for me.

"Good morning, Luna."

"Good morning, Clyde. I wanted to stop in and see if you were alright." I replied, stepping in so he could close the door.

"I am. I appreciate your concern. I'm just cleaning things up in here."

I looked across the room, finding a few chairs still knocked over.

"Let me help you."

"Thank you, Luna. I don't want to be an inconvenience."

"Not at all."

I took off my coat and hung it from one of the chairs by the door before walking further into the bar and beginning to pick up the chairs.

"Usually, we clean up before we leave for the night, but we didn't have a chance after all of last night's drama."

"I'm sorry that happened to you," I said sympathetically.

"We're wolves," he laughed. "A few skirmishes are bound to happen."

I nodded in understanding and continued with the work. It only took us an hour or so to complete everything. I brushed off my hands and looked at our efforts. You wouldn't ever have known that there was a fight here last night.

"Thank you for all of your help, Luna. I need to get going for my community service."

"Community service?"

"Yes, my punishment for fighting last night," he said with a knowing smile.

"Oh, makes sense, I guess."

I assumed they broke the fight up and sent them to cool off. I hadn't realized that Forest had given them consequences for it, though it didn't surprise me after he had wanted to execute Sienna six months ago for simply insulting me.

"Well, good luck."

"Thanks, I appreciate your help this morning."

He walked me out and locked up behind us before

heading towards the barracks. I turned and continued on my way down Main Street, leaving it behind as I went to the gardens. In the fall, I convinced Forest to build a greenhouse so that we could keep fresh herbs and plants over winter. He erected a large twenty-foot one just in time to move many of the plants indoors before the frost came. I could hear Oliver inside and open the glass door.

"Hi, Oliver; how has the greenhouse held up over the week?"

"She's done just fine, Luna," he smiled back at me. "I had to turn the heaters up with the storm on Tuesday, but she fared well."

"Thank you for taking care of it for me."

"Not a problem."

Oliver and the other garden workers usually had winters off. Some of them picked up work in the town or helped with the animals, but Oliver took it off and spent that time with his mate. He had been helping me take care of the greenhouse on the odd days I couldn't make it, but it was fairly easy work. Temperatures must be monitored, and the plants need watering every few days.

"Why don't you head out? I can take over from here," I told him.

"Thank you, Luna."

He passed me the watering can and grabbed his coat from a protruding nail near the door. I finished off the can and went back outside to the hand pump. It was fed from an underground water stream—one of the reasons the garden had been built in this area.

With the departure of the Silver Ridge Pack, my routine was returning to normal. I cared for the greenhouse and helped around the pack where I could. Forest would be busy catching up on work the next few days, so I would be mostly on my own. I had considered heading up to the lake after I had finished here, but with the shortened days, I knew it would be too close to sunset by the time I made the trip. Instead, I found my way back to our apartment and settled in for an evening of movies.

12

Juniper

I plopped on the chair across from Forest as he worked on reviewing the monthly reports. So many reports. You would think that they wouldn't need everything documented in such a detailed manner, but Forest was adamant that the pack kept up with them. He said it was a way to ensure that the pack ran smoothly. He also reminded me of my attempts to pull him away and that the records were of how we had found my father.

"So, with the full moon next week, I was thinking that I would head down to my coven so that I could celebrate with them."

He stopped what he was doing and looked up at me with a combative expression.

"I can't make it down next week. I need to be here for the pack run. There have been a few rogues in the area. We talked about this already."

"I know. I feel the need to go down there. I told you my

power has not been fully restored since we were there three months ago. I need to go," I said more sternly.

"You cannot go by yourself."

Frustration swelled within me at his denial, but I knew that if I turned this to anger, I would have no chance of convincing him.

"What if you take me down a few days before and pick me up after?" I offered.

"I'm uncomfortable with you being there unprotected," he said with a firm tone.

I attempted to reassure him, "I lived my whole life there before you without anything happening. I will be fine."

"No," he replied sternly.

At his blatant refusal, the anger that I had been stifling down burned with a renewed vengeance.

"You cannot keep me here, Forest. You can come with me, or you can let me go on my own. But either way, I am going."

Usually, I would listen to him if he had concerns, but he could be an overbearing ass with his protective nature. He hated it when I went to the lake on my own, even though it was on pack territory, and now he refused to let me visit my family, my coven! I had offered for him to take me, but even that, he seemed to be against it. I would not back down from this argument. It was unfair and unfounded.

I was sure he sensed my growing emotions. I watched him with a hawk-like stare as he rubbed his forehead in agitation before running his hand down his face,

"August and four other warriors will go with you," he finally countered.

"My coven had a hard enough time letting you in. Do you really think that they would let others intrude?"

"If there's no protection, there is no going."

"Forest, please. This is important."

He sighed, "Fine...August and the others will take you down. They will stay in town. If there is the slightest hint of trouble, you will link them so they can get there quickly. If you leave the settlement, they must be with you."

"Deal!" I said excitedly. "We will leave on Saturday so I can spend time with my family before the celebration."

"I will let the others know."

I jumped up and ran around his desk to kiss him deeply before racing upstairs to call my Gran. I rummaged through the desk, unplugged my cell, and pressed her contact.

"Hello," she answered; the sounds of the others were chaotic in the background. I could hear her pull the phone to the side so that she could hear better.

"Gran, it's Juniper."

"Oh, hi. I'm surprised to hear from you so early."

"I wanted to call with some news," I said excitedly.

"What's that, my sweet girl?"

"I am coming home for a visit!"

"That's wonderful! When will you two be here?" she asked.

"It will just be me. Forest can't get away. I'm coming down on Saturday. I plan on staying for the full moon. I need a good recharge."

"I'm sure you do. I have wondered how you have faired without the coven."

I sighed, "I've tried doing the rituals on my own, but it's like lighting a candle compared to a bonfire."

"You will learn to pull in more of Selene's energy independently. I am glad to have you here, though," she replied knowingly.

"Me too. I will see you in three days."

"See you in three days, Juniper. I will let the coven know of your return."

"Thanks, Gran. I love you."

"I love you too, dear."

IT HAD BEEN MORE challenging than I thought to say goodbye to Forest. The bond twisted inside me at the impending separation, and the further we drove away from the pack, the harder it became. The bond pulled on me as if telling me I was going the wrong way, but I knew how much I wanted to see my coven, so I pushed on. August drove Forest's car down while the other three followed in one of the pack vehicles. The four-hour drive felt immensely longer while suffering from the separation. When we pulled up near the drive to the coven, August hopped out, giving me the car.

"I have my cell phone if you cannot link me," he told me, holding the driver's door open for me to climb in.

"Okay. I'll let you know if we plan on going anywhere, but I would be surprised if we did."

"Yes, Luna," he replied while bowing his head.

He always spoke so officially, even though I considered him a friend. I would drive in on my own the remaining distance since there was a ward to repel unwelcome visitors, and they would return to town. They would be staying in the only motel there. August and the others waited for me to turn down the dirt drive and disappear among the thick forest before turning around and heading back into town. I squeezed the SUV down the narrow path, finally bringing it to a halt alongside the other cars parked at the settlement. The sleek black Range Rover starkly contrasted the older vehicles alongside it. I could already see a few of the women running down to greet me. At the front was Meadow, waving like the crazy woman she was. She nearly ripped me out of the vehicle and pulled me against her in a tight hug.

"Juniper! I am so glad you're here!" she excitedly said.

"Hey Meadow, I am too," I hugged her back.

"Hi, Juniper," Cedar Heenan, another one of my friends, said as she followed Meadow up to me.

"Hey, how are you?"

"Same old, same old. You know," she replied light-heartedly.

I carried my bag up the pathway, greeting each person I passed until we arrived at my family's home, the Nary house. The snow contrasting against dark timber planks rising from their stone foundation was a welcomed sight that I had missed. I loved the West Moon Pack and all the buildings there, but the nostalgia of returning to my child-hood home could not be beaten. We pushed the heavy wood door open, and heat warmed my cheeks as we entered.

"Juniper," my Gran called as she exited the kitchen.

She walked up to me and hugged me tightly, as grand-mothers do. In one tight hold of her arms, I felt comfort and all things soothing.

"I am so glad to see you."

"I'm glad to be back."

Violet, my great aunt, walked in behind her, "I was unsure if you would be here for the cold moon. As a member of the Whisper Creek coven and as a witch, you know how important it is for us."

My Aunt Violet was one for order and cutting straight to the point. She was the eldest of us and the unofficial leader, though she held the highest ranking among the other elders. The eldest member of each of the six families of the settlement sat as an elder and was the governing group for our coven. They were the ones who made all of the rules and decisions.

"I knew I needed to be here," I smiled at her, not worrying about the harshness in her voice.

It was nothing more than typical Violet. She walked up to me, held my chin in her hand, and examined my face.

"You have let your power dwindle," she said dryly.

"It has been difficult to hold the full moon ceremony alone.'

"This is why we stay together," her tone was stern.

"I know, but you know how the mate bond works."

She hummed at me, unconvinced. They had granted me their blessing to stay a part of the coven even while I resided at the pack, but it was far more than they would have considered for anyone else under any other circumstances.

She released my face, "you can help prepare for dinner."

"I would love to," I replied, knowing she was trying to prove her position over me.

Just because I was a Luna at the pack, I had not earned the privilege of rank at the coven. It would stay that way until I, too, became an elder. I watched as she turned for her study, leaving us alone. Gran took my hand and led us to the kitchen.

"Don't mind her. She has been cranky lately. You know how she gets."

I let out a small chuckle, "I sure do."

"I'm making forest stew for you."

My excitement grew at her announcement of my favorite meal for dinner.

"What can I do?"

"You can cut up the mushrooms."

I sat on one of the stools near the counter and pulled over the wooden board and bowl filled to the rim with Pacific golden chanterelle mushrooms. Meadow sat on the stool next to me and began to shuck the peas from their pods while Gran returned to her pan of rabbit meat that she was sautéing. We laughed as we caught up on the latest happenings in our lives. It was small moments like these that I missed at the pack house.

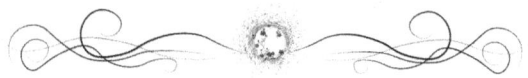

13

Juniper

I rolled the ball of snow across the meadow with my mittened hands, slowly building its girth. When it reached the desired size, I pulled it into my arms and carried it over to the other one I had already placed. I carefully set it on top of the other and packed some snow around the middle, ensuring they held together. Meadow added another smaller ball to the stack, completing our snowman.

"There, now all we need is some sticks and rocks," she said putting her fists on her hips in a look of accomplishment.

We walked over to the tree line in search of some branches. The snow was thick and heavy, making it difficult to walk. We dug around the base of some trees until we found our desired items. We then walked back over, adding two arms, some pebble eyes, a twig nose, a row of rocks for a mouth, and a few for its buttons.

"Now for the finishing touches," she said, reaching into

her satchel. She pulled out a brightly colored wrap that she wound around the neck, followed by a dried flower crown that she placed on top of its head.

"She's beautiful."

I looked at her, holding her fists up to her chin just as a child would.

"The crown was a nice touch," I winked at her.

"Well, you can't leave a girl without a crown," she gawked.

"Of course not," I laughed back.

"Maybe we can find her some hair? We could use some pine branches, although I don't want to give her a bad hair-do," she said as she leaned back, inspecting our snow-woman with her fist at her chin.

I bent over in a fit of laughter, clutching my stomach.

"What?" she asked defensively.

I laughed harder, unable to contain it.

"You make me laugh, Meadow. You even doll up your snowmen."

"Excuse me, *Snowwoman*," she scolded me with a hand on her hip.

Another fit of laughter burst from me. That was until I felt the icy impact of snow hitting the side of my head. I stood up with a shocked but playful face.

"It's on now, Meadow," I said as I dove my mittens into the snow, grabbing a chunk and rolling it into a tight ball.

We began an epic battle of snow, hurtling it at one another. The ordinarily silent meadow was filled with our screams and laughter as we partook in our childish game. My arm was pulled back, ready to throw my latest ammunition against my best friend, when I felt pressure pushing on my back. I whipped around, looking for the source, finding nothing but crisp air behind me.

"Don't mind that," Meadow said, walking up to me.

"What do you mean?" I asked, surprised.

"Someone's been hanging out north of us, and they keep getting too close to the ward," she explained.

"There's no one to the north of us. It's just forest," I questioned, surprised by the lack of her concern.

"The elders think there may be some campers up there."

"It's winter. No campers would be out right now," I pushed, not satisfied with her answer.

She shrugged, "They haven't made it past the ward, so we aren't worried."

Maybe it was from my time at the pack, but it didn't feel right. My wolf bristled inside of me, confirming my suspicions.

"Has anyone been up to check it out?"

She laughed, "Like anyone here would go all that way out in the snow just to spy on some campers or hikers wandering around."

"Maybe I should check it out," I said, looking to the north.

"You know it's like two and a half miles from here. Considering how deep the snow is already, that will take you at least an hour, maybe even more. They will be long gone by the time you get there."

I smirked at her, "I can shift, remember. My wolf is much faster."

"What will you do, scare the living daylights out of them by showing them a wolf? What if they're hunting? You could be a prized catch for them. It's not worth it, Juniper," she said, shaking her head.

I reluctantly gave up on the idea of going out to investigate further. We decided that we would instead return home to warm our bodies, more for Meadow than for me. We trudged our way back to the settlement through the deep blanket of gleaming snow. I could not get the ward situation out of my head. It had happened on the rare occasion when I still lived within the coven, but something felt off this time. Meadow had made it seem like whoever was pushing our borders had done so multiple times. When I had experienced it before, it would be a single time, never repeating.

"How many times has the ward been pushed?"

"I don't know...it's been happening a couple of times a day for the last few weeks," she explained dully.

I stopped and grabbed her hand, making her look at me.

"And no one has gone out to look into it?" I asked seriously.

"They decided to leave them be. It is a long trek through poor conditions. They put up a secondary ward closer to the settlement for assurance. We were right near it in the meadow."

While they had at least done something, I still disliked the situation. Something in my gut told me there was more to it. I could see that even Meadow seemed unfazed, so I let the conversation die, but it still stormed within my thoughts.

Meadow was shivering by the time we walked in the door. A fire burned in the hearth, and she nearly ran over to it, stripping off her wet wool mittens and beginning to warm her fingers.

"What on earth have you two been doing to become so wet?" Gran asked as she walked into the room.

"Nothing," Meadow replied defensively.

"I don't believe you one bit, Meadow Nary," Gran bit back at her. "You better warm up quickly. Your mom wants you to head home to wash the dishes. She's been at it all morning. Some new 'silken skin' product she's come up with."

Meadow threw her head back, "Gah, not again. Does she realize there are other people here that can do that? What about Wren? She's home."

"Your sister is resting. You know her pregnancy hasn't been easy on her. And from what I've heard from Violet, she has been doing more than her fair share."

In defeat, Meadow squished her face together before looking at me, "So what do you say? Want to help a girl out?"

"No, can do," my Gran responded. "I've volunteered Juniper to help me make the centerpieces for tomorrow."

"What? It's the cold moon...they're not even hard to make," Meadow sulked.

"You would know what went into them if you ever volunteered to help out," Gran bantered back at her.

I shrugged my shoulders at her and smiled, "I'll check on you when I'm done. If you are still at it, I will help."

"Thanks..." she sighed before tightening her coat around her and leaving the house.

They lived in a house next door, but it was still a few minutes walk to get there.

"So, centerpieces, huh?" I asked Gran as she went for her coat.

"I thought it would help you connect for the celebration a little deeper. There is a reason why we put so much effort into it."

"I know, it's something to be celebrated."

"Not just that," she said as we started walking to the main hall, "We bring items that help us connect to Selene. Tonight, we bring silver candles for the moon and gold for the sun. We celebrate the longest night and the rebirth of the warmth, always in balance."

We entered the main hall and took a seat at one of the

tables that had been set up. An array of materials were piled in the center. A few more women followed us in before Daisy Martin stood from her chair.

"Alright, ladies, you know what to do. I have a sample of what we will be making on my table. Take your time studying it so as not to miss any of the details. Now let's get to work."

Daisy was the primary coordinator for all of our celebrations. She had a natural knack for event planning. She was organized, detail-oriented, and good at leading a group. Gran and I stood and walked over, joining the others, looking over the stunning centerpiece. Thin wooden boards were laid across white linen. A mirror, just smaller than the board, was placed on top. Several styles of vases filled with clear water ran down the center and were surrounded by various white and gold candles with evergreen branches and winterberries woven throughout.

Once we had taken a good look, we returned to our seats and began on our first centerpiece. I pushed the materials to the side and laid the wool down, followed by the board. Gran gently placed the mirror on top.

"The mirror is for reflection. Reflection of the moonlight and reflection of one's self."

I smiled and nodded at her, wondering why she was getting into so much detail about the meaning of everything. I placed the vases down in the center.

"Water is a great source of energy for us. It stores it from the moon."

"Okay, Gran," I said, going along with whatever she was doing.

We placed the candles around the outside of the vases and filled in the fresh, evergreen beaches. With a finishing touch, we added a pop of color with winterberry and finished our first one. I carefully picked it up and carried it to a table set aside for the fished products. When I returned, Gran had already laid the wool and wood down. I picked up the mirror, placing it in its place.

"Reflection. It is an important thing to strengthen your intuition. You must learn to trust yourself," she explained further.

I eyed her suspiciously, "Why are you going on about all this, Gran? I remember what each item means. We were taught this in our lessons."

She reached across the table, taking my hands within hers, "When you thank Selene for her gift and offer yourself to her at the full moon, it is more than just the words. It is about taking the time to show her your devotion. Each full moon is filled with a different meaning. Little pieces begin to chip away without giving each meaning its place within you. We can survive without them but are much more powerful with them."

I stared at her in awed reverence. Until I left, these little things were part of my daily life. I never thought much about why we did them beyond the basic symbolism they stood for.

"Thank you," I said full-heartedly.

I now knew why she had volunteered me for this. I needed to know how to feel more fulfilled when I could not travel to the coven for the full moon. There were two parts of me, both with requirements, and it was up to me to learn to balance them. I needed to know how to care for myself without relying so heavily on my coven.

I took special care with each placement and listened intently to all the wisdom my Gran bestowed upon me that night. If I were to find balance in my life, I would need all the help and knowledge I could gather from her.

14

Juniper

With a greater appreciation for the preparations for the full moon celebration, I happily volunteered the following morning for the setup. We used the same evergreen branches used for the centerpieces and wrapped them around a rope strung between posts along with a braided and draped silver ribbon. We cleared the snow from the ground so our bare feet would not be entrapped in its icy embrace while we danced around the fire. Even with the added body heat that my wolf supplied me, I was still thankful that the bonfire was lit early, sending waves of warmth to comfort me.

Halfway through our preparations, I felt the ward being pushed once again. We stopped briefly, all eyes to the north until the pressure disappeared. The swirl of caution ate at my gut as the others returned to their work. I was still in disbelief that they did not take a greater interest in what was happening. I felt like I needed to talk to Violet about this. Perhaps there was more to it than was being let on.

Once we were done, I returned to the house to help my Gran with her cooking. On my way to the kitchen, I saw Violet in her office.

I stepped inside, "Do you have a minute, Aunt Violet?"

"I do," she answered, looking up at me.

I sat down on one of the chairs opposite her.

"Why have you not investigated the ward disturbances yet?"

She sat back in her chair and looked intently at me as if attempting to read my mind.

"This bothers you," she said as a statement rather than a question.

"It does. Something about it doesn't feel right. I think someone should go out and check on it," I urged her.

She was silent for a minute as she contemplated my concerns.

"This year has been difficult for the weather. It is a difficult journey," she explained monotone.

"That shouldn't matter. If something keeps going at the ward, it could only be a matter of time before it gets through," I pushed.

She stood from her chair and walked around her desk. She carefully closed the door and returned to her seat.

"We have sent a pair of women out to look into it," she attempted to reassure me.

"What did they see? Did they see these supposed campers Meadow told me about?"

"No. All that they found were some animal tracks."

Her expression held little concern for the situation, which worried me. These types of situations should be held at the highest importance.

"Animals don't set off the ward," I told her.

She already knew that. We would not feel the ward push

if it were an animal. It had to be something more, whether a human or...something else.

"Dangerous ones do. It protects us from any person or creature that would harm us," she frowned at my questioning.

"But why would a creature keep coming back? They have never done that before. The consistency is alarming. "

"We are unsure. We have strengthened the ward and have cast several others as a precaution. After the women returned, the disturbances increased. We do not want whatever is at our borders to be further enticed to come inside; therefore, we are keeping our distance."

"Why did you not tell me sooner? Perhaps the pack could help," I offered.

"We have survived here for over one hundred years without the need of others," she scowled at my suggestion. "The world takes as it gives; if we were to ask for help, then your pack may come to us with demands in the future."

"That is just stubbornness speaking. We are family."

"You are family," she said curtly, "they are not. What is to say that your pack members would not start traveling down to us asking for spells to help aid all their ailments?"

"They wouldn't do that," I argued back.

"But they could."

"Anyone could."

"No, because they do not know where we are, what we are capable of," she argued.

I squeezed my fists together to stop myself from bickering with her further.

"What if this creature gets past the ward? You don't even know what it is," I asked, returning the conversation to the matter.

"We are a powerful coven and will do what we must," she said sternly.

I shook my head in frustration.

She looked me over and said, "You may disagree with us on this matter, but the decision is up to us to make. I believe we are at the end of our conversation."

Her unsubtle hint that it was time for me to leave her office was taken. I pursed my lips and forced a nod of appreciation for her time before leaving. I took a deep breath before deciding to look for my Gran. I knew she was cooking and needed something to take my mind off the conversation with Violet.

When I walked into the kitchen, she was preparing the red current cake and a venison stew for the feast that would be served. Each household would make several dishes to share with the others. For the cold moon, a handful of ingredients were focused on, such as nuts, cinnamon, and currants. My Gran had offered to make two currant dishes; she had been at it all morning. It was quite a feat, making enough to feed our coven of over ninety women, but family meals were typical here, so most only had to multiply their serving by six to feed the other families.

When the dishes were ready, I helped carry them down to the gathering before returning to get prepared. One of the good things about these celebrations was that you never had to worry about an outfit, not that we ever did anyway. None of the women here wore makeup or fancy clothes. Instead, we mainly dressed in handmade clothing and took a more natural approach to our appearance. We had no one to impress but instead embraced our femininity and the natural beauty from within. Heavy, thin, old, young...we were all the same.

I stripped off my clothes and let my hair down from its ponytail, running my fingers through it to straighten the curls a bit. I grabbed my black cloak that still hung on the back of my door and wrapped it over my shoulders, tying it around my neck. I pulled the hood over my head and returned downstairs, finding the others already gathering near the door. While in summer, we would walk barefoot down to the bonfire, in winter, we would wear our boots for the walk, storing them under the tables once we had arrived. I slipped my black winter boots on and hooked Meadow's arm.

"I'm glad to be here with you," I smiled at her.

"I know, I'm the best," she said as she threw her hair over her shoulder.

I laughed and pushed my shoulder into hers. We began the walk through the trees and down to the center of the settlement. The raging bonfire lit the space in a warm yellow glow. The tables were lit by candles displaying all of the food that had been made. I smiled when I saw our handy work in the center of the tables. The vases had been filled with water, harnessing the moon's energy. We took our seats and filled our plates.

"Aren't you a sight for sore eyes," Clover, another of my old friends, said as we approached.

I hugged her, "I could say the same about you."

"So, how's married life?" she asked with a mischievous smile.

"I'm not married," I corrected her.

"Close enough. Do shifters even get married?"

"Not really. They mate, as they call it."

"So what does that entail?'

My cheeks blushed at the memory of when Forest and I first mated, "You know."

Both Meadow and Clover giggled, and I felt myself blushing.

"No, I think you need to tell us," Clover smirked at me.

"Yeah, all the details," Meadow added.

"You're not going to get that from me."

"I've seen what your mate looks like. We all have," Meadow cooed, "I know what I would do to him if I could."

I fought a growl as jealousy began to burn within me, a side effect of my shifter half. We were fiercely territorial over our mates. Even a comment made in good fun could send someone over the edge, or so I heard. I had to bite my lip not to throw an insult out in retaliation for her words.

"I have learned how protective mates are, even of words," I sent her a warning look.

Meadow held her hands up, "Sorry, I didn't mean anything by it."

She rolled her head back, "I'm just envious. I wish I could find a shifter of my own."

I released my fist that had clenched, letting go of my wild feelings.

"I'm sorry, Meadow," I said, referring to my reaction and her wish to be with a man.

She had always loved the romance movies in the theater, but it was never something that would happen for us, or so we thought, until I met Forest. We had accepted it, but I feared that I had changed that with my relationship. It was as if I had set a new precedent that there could be a chance. Guilt began to fill my chest the more I thought about it.

"Come on, you two," Clover interrupted, "I spy some cinnamon rolls that are calling our names."

I was thankful for the redirection. We dove into the feast, and the conversation turned more lighthearted. We laughed and talked until it was time for the ceremony to start. We all circled the flames as Violet stepped forward, raising her hands to the moon.

"*Le deireadh do chuairt, bheir sinn ar blàths thugad*," she chanted before dropping her robe, revealing her naked body.

We each followed her lead, chanting as we, too, dropped our robes. As if on cue, the ward pushed on us from the north, yet this time, no one looked to see. They were too focused on the ceremony to give it the caution that they should. I looked around, catching Violet's eye as she gave me a slight shake of her head, telling me to let it go. I huffed out a hard breath but did as she said. Instead, I focused on the chant and the moon. As we began dancing around the fire, I could feel the moon's power surge into my body, filling me in ways I had failed to achieve on my own. We frolicked and swayed as the spiked wassail was passed out, warming us from the inside. Where before, I would find myself quickly overtaken by the alcoholic treat, my new fortitude kept it at bay, yet it did not stop me from enjoying myself and my family.

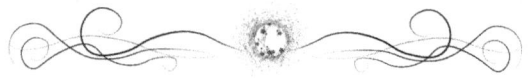

15

Juniper

With the cold kissed wind nipping at our bare bodies, the celebration ended earlier than the ones that happened in the warmer months. Meadow was utterly inebriated, so I helped her get to her house and tucked her into bed. I exited her room and found Heather, her mom, sitting at the dining room table.

"How are you doing, Juniper?" she asked solemnly.

When I first found Forest, I was on a trip for Heather's business with her and Meadow. She used a compulsion charm, a forbidden spell, on me to force me to leave. I was lucky that Forest was able to save me. The coven left it to me to decide whether she should be exiled due to her use of the spell, but I chose to spare her. I loved her, but all the trust I had in her was gone.

"I'm good. How are you?"

"I'm good too. I'm glad to see you back here," her former boisterous confidence had transformed into shy and timid, as if she didn't know how to talk to me anymore.

"Yeah, me too."

She stood up and placed her tea mug in her kitchen sink. I watched her movements as she made her way towards the hall.

"Well, goodnight."

"Goodnight," I responded as she went down to her bedroom.

Ever since all of that had happened, it was awkward between us. It was like neither of us knew what to say to the other. I walked over to the Nary house, our family home, and pulled off my cape again, draping it over one of the old wooden rocking chairs on the front porch. All night, my wolf had been calling to me, as she did every full moon. Just as my witch side needed to connect with Selene, so did my wolf. I tucked my boots against the wall, walked into the small front garden, and shifted into my petite framed red wolf. I stretched my front paws out before shaking my fur. I trotted away from the house and the settlement, weaving through the trees to my favorite meadow. It was the same one that Meadow and I had built the snowman in only yesterday. It still stood at the center, surrounded by the disturbed snow.

Running as my wolf alone felt no more right than pulling Selene's power from the full moon alone as I did at the pack. Though I enjoyed my independence, both halves of my life were nourished by community and connection. I decided that even though Forest, who I was missing terribly at that moment, was not here, I still had the others who had accompanied me. They had taken themselves away from the pack run in order to keep me safe. I was grateful for them, even if it was an order by their alpha.

August, are you around?

Yes, Luna. We are running through the woods between the coven and the town.

I'll come to join you.

It would be an honor, Luna.

I laughed internally at his chivalry. Just as I turned to meet up with them, I felt the wards's pressure again. It was much stronger than before. I knew I could not let this go ignored any further. If the pressure was that great, then something was attempting to cross. I needed to check it out.

I'll be a little bit. I need to check in on something, I told August before racing North.

I had considered having them come with me, but they would not be allowed past the ward and would have to circle, putting them in the same space as whatever the disturbance was. On the other hand, I could be shielded by the ward's protection.

The still forest, lit only by the white glow of the full moon, was filled with the smell of damp pine and a crunching sound as I stepped across the frozen blanket beneath me. All the animals that called these woods their home were tightly tucked in their burrows, protected from the frosty air. I raced for the first two miles, moving quickly to minimize the time it would take to reach the outer boundary. It was easy to navigate the dense winter wonderland in my nimble form. My petite frame and light-footed step allowed me to move quickly through the hidden obstacles. When I could feel the ward approaching, I decided to cast an invisibility spell upon myself so as not to show whatever was nearby my presence. I had never cast a spell while in my wolf form, but I figured I would try it so I did not need to shift first.

I imagined my body in both forms, focusing my

thoughts on it. I moved my head as if tracing my outlines and began to say my incantation within my mind.

"*Thig còmhla rium leis na ballachan agus na speuran. Dèan mi neo-fhaicsinneach don t-sùil.*"

When my eyes opened, I was thrilled to find it had worked! Pleased with myself, I pushed forward, stepping lightly to make the minimal amount of sound possible. With the edge of the ward in my sight, I crouched and inched forward. I could see the tell tail signs of tracks of some animal pacing back and forth along the ward. Something definitely knew that it was there and was testing the boundary. I found a fallen log to hide behind to see if I could catch sight of it.

I waited for nearly an hour without sighting this mysterious creature. I decided to relent in my surveillance and join August and the others. They were most likely wondering where I was anyway.

Are you still to the East of me? I asked him.

Yes, Luna.

Okay, I am at our north border. I will head your way now.

Yes, Luna.

I stood up, giving my legs a quick moment to regain their feeling, when I heard a heavy crunch in front of me. I dropped back down, my eyes intently scouring the forest in that direction. The crunching sound continued, moving closer to me. I held my breath in anticipation. The shadows danced within the trees, tipping off my eyes to the movement. The wind shifted in my direction, giving me the horrid scent of rot. There was more to it, though; I could tell it was a creature, but almost as if it had slept in a rotting carcass overnight. I knew the scent of all the creatures that lived in the forest, having come upon them in my time at the pack, and none had the same underlying smell that this had. My wolf's hackles raised at the incoming threat. Using her instincts, I knew that whatever was approaching me was dangerous. I couldn't move. I did not want to alert it of my presence.

Just as my mind raced through all of the possibilities, the imposing figure broke through the dark shield of the deep forest and stepped into the moonlight. I gasped at the horrendous sight in front of me. I had never seen or even heard of a creature such as this. It looked like an amalgam of many animals, some disturbed scientist's monstrous creation. Its hind legs resembled my wolf's but stood upright like a man. Its torso looked emancipated, deathly thin with protruding ribs. Instead of paws, it was held up by twisted hoofed feet. Its long arms came down to its knees with long, terrifying claws. The head, hunched over its shoulders on a long fur-covered neck, looked like an elk with large branch-like antlers jutting in all directions but with a mouth full of jagged teeth with visible drool slipping its way down the jaw. This creature was built from nightmares. It was not natural in any sense of the word. My small wolf was dwarfed by its nearly eight-foot height.

I stood no chance against this creature. I needed to stay hidden until it retreated to where it came from. It walked to the edge of the ward and raised its head as a wolf would do to howl. Instead of a howl or grunt, as I would have expected, a long whistling sound came out, as if the wind whistled through the trees, but there was no mistaking the source. When the creature's head lowered, it looked right at me.

I looked back down at myself, still finding my invisible form. I was downwind, so it should not have been able to scent me. How had it known where I was? Was it just a coincidence? It crouched down, never taking its dark, soulless eyes off of my direction. I tucked myself further behind the log, hiding as best I could.

"Help..." a ghostly woman's voice called out.

My head darted up, looking for the source of the cry. With horror, I realized that it was the creature who made the call. The snow beneath my feet crushed down as I shifted my weight, and the monster whistled into the air again before running in my direction. I turned and ran as fast as I could away from it. I could feel the ward's pressure push, and I glanced back, seeing it still pushing toward me as if it were fighting the invisible barrier.

I wasted no time as I flew through the woods, gaining as much distance as possible. Just as I thought I had escaped the monstrosity's pursuit, I felt the ward crumble. My feet stumbled as fear pierced my heart. I realized it had made it past the protection of magic and was now on settlement land. I could hear the faint sound of its footfalls gaining as it chased me through the forest. My legs burned as I pushed myself harder than I ever had before. The terrifying creature was closing in too quickly.

I felt myself pass through one of the additional wards the elders had cast, which gave me a sense of relief. I ran just a little further before spotting a hollowed-out trunk up ahead. I dove in, hiding myself away. As the creature's footsteps approached the second ward, I held my breath, remaining perfectly still. The haunting whistle echoed through the forest, and I could hear it pacing. I dared not move. I could not risk revealing myself once more. If it were to break this ward, I would have to run away from the settlement. It would be my only chance to lure it away from the others.

The continued crunching sound felt like it lasted forever before it finally retreated into the woods. I waited a while longer before slowly peering out. There was no sign of it. I moved as silently as possible until I felt myself pass through the third and final ward that had been placed. With the added protection and knowledge of the distance between us, my mind returned to August and the others. They were in the woods with the creature.

August, I shouted through the link.

Luna, what's wrong? He asked concerned.

You need to go back to the town! Stay in your motel room.

Why? What's happened?

There is some type of monster in the forest. The ward has broken, I shouted through the link.

We are coming to you.

No. I need you to listen to me. We have more wards in place, but you need to go back to the motel now, I said forcefully.

We must protect you, he said adamantly.

I am protected, but you are not. You would not even be able to get to me. Go back to the motel. I will speak to the elders and ask them to grant you entry, I attempted to reassure him.

I could tell he was hesitant, but he finally agreed. Now that I knew the pack would be safe, I could focus on the coven. They needed to be warned.

16

Juniper

I ran through the center of the settlement, finding the main hall illuminated and the sound of voices coming from within. I turned towards it, shifting along the way. I paused and released my invisibility spell before entering. All voices halted at my sudden intrusion. I looked around; the entire coven had gathered, their faces filled with concern and worry.

"Juniper..." Gran stood near the front, looking over my naked and disheveled appearance. "What has happened to you?"

"There is a monster in the woods."

"What are you speaking of Juniper? What have you done?" Violet asked accusingly.

"I went for a run as my wolf. I was drawn to the north border," I told them.

"I warned you to stay away," she seethed at me.

"I know you did, but I needed to know. Something is not right about it," I tried to explain.

"That does not matter. You went against my orders," she fumed.

"Is that not what the cold moon is about? This is a time of self-reflection, a time to connect with our instincts and beliefs within them. I knew that there was something more to the ward being pushed. I trusted my intuition and knew that something dangerous was out there," I challenged her. "I was not ignorant in my approach. I cast an invisibility spell, and even then, I stayed hidden behind a fallen log."

"What did you see?" my Gran asked, standing up from her seat.

"I have never seen something like it. It was giant and looked like a mix of an elk, a wolf, and a man. It could see or at least sense me even through the invisibility spell. Whatever it is, it's dangerous; it knows we are here. It will not stop until it gets in."

Gasps of fear spread through the women seated around me.

"It was your reckless actions that have brought it to us," Violet accused.

"That is not true, and you know it, Mom." Heather stood, defending me. "The ward was being pushed weeks before her arrival. It had already been increasing. This was not of her doing. She was the only one brave enough to find an answer."

Sounds of agreement murmured from the crowd. Violet's rage burned in her eyes.

"Even so, her actions tonight have brought down the ward."

"Then you did the right thing by adding the others," I told her.

"Others?" Another girl asked. "I thought you added only one."

Violet pursed her lips together, "We added two for security."

"So all this time that you told us that it was merely campers, you also had your worries?" Heather asked her accusingly.

"We did not know what it was. We only knew it was a creature."

"That is not campers, Mom," Heather said sternly. "We trust the elders to be honest with us and protect us. You decided for us."

"We did not deceive you; we tried to protect you," Pearl, the elder from the Murphy family, added.

"What would have happened if this creature broke through before we had a warning? We could have been attacked!" Heather continued to argue.

"That is why we put additional wards in place. We would have had plenty of time to prepare."

"Not enough," Heather stated.

"I know you all don't believe in letting others in," I interjected. "I would like to ask some of my pack members to come onto coven lands."

"Why would we do that?" Violet asked angrily.

"They have been staying in the town, and I would like them to be protected within our wards."

"You brought pack members down with you?" she asked accusingly.

"Just as we travel in pairs, they sent them to protect me for my stay here. They have made no attempt to come on our lands. I would feel better if they were here, protected from the creature. Besides, they would protect us if something more were to happen with the creature."

"We do not allow outsiders to stay with us," Violet yelled, surprising the room at her outburst.

I didn't shy away from her temper, "They are my pack, just like a coven. They are a part of me, and I am asking you for this."

"You are barely a coven member yourself these days. This is only the fourth time we have seen you in half a year!" Violet eyed me with disdain.

"You dare not speak of my granddaughter that way! She is a part of this coven, and you know it," Gran spat at her. "Besides, it is not up to just you. This must be a coven decision. We will put it to a vote."

Several others around Gran shouted their agreement.

"Fine, what say you sisters? Shall we allow these outsiders into our sacred, protected lands? But I warn thee, it is a slippery slope. If we do it once, nothing will stop them from asking again."

"And we would vote then as well," I added.

Violet grumbled at me.

"All those in favor?" She asked the room, her disapproval heavy in her tone.

Hand after hand raised, followed by their 'aye's.'

"All those opposed?" She raised her hand, the only one of a noticeable minority.

"I feel like this is a grave mistake, but your pack members may enter," she said with reservation.

I felt a sense of accomplishment. Violet had always been stubborn in her ways, though her insult of my position in the coven stung deeply.

"Now we must decide what to do with this creature, the real matter at hand. For the time being, we will cast additional wards as an added barrier between us. With any luck, it will move on with time. Until then, we practice both our offensive and defensive spells. All of you are required to attend," she looked across the room, her anger still evident. "Now return to your homes."

The crowd began to filter out of the hall.

August, you and the others can stay at the coven. I will meet you at the drive.

We are on our way, he replied.

My Gran pulled me in tightly to her, "You were a brave girl tonight. We all can thank you for following your intuition. We now have time to prepare for whatever haunts the woods."

"Thank you for opening my eyes to it."

She smiled and kissed my cheek, "I will see you at home."

I smiled and nodded before she walked away. I still had no clothes, so I decided to shift and meet the others at the drive. I was shaken from my encounter but felt secure enough to travel as I was still within the protective wards. I trotted down the main drive, tonight's events tangled in a whirlwind in my mind. When I approached the road, I stepped into the bushes nearby, waiting for my pack's arrival. When I heard the wind blowing at my back, I whipped around, expecting to see the creature again, but all I found were the rustling branches of the conifers.

The blinding lights of a car approaching caught my attention. I watched as it pulled off the road in the same place they had left me days before. The driver's door opened, but I could not make out what existed behind the lights, so I waited. August walked around the vehicle, illuminating himself. My wolf walked out of the brush, revealing myself to him.

He bowed his head to me, "Luna."

I walked up to him. Ridge, another one of the men, stepped out and laid an oversized shirt on the ground in front of me. They each turned their backs as I shifted, slipping the shirt over my head.

"Thank you for coming," I told them.

"What happened tonight, Luna?" August asked.

The other three men stepped out to join our conversation.

"There have been disturbances in our ward for the last few weeks. Something has been trying to get in. I went to check it out, and I found..." I stalled as the memory of the horrific beast returned to my memory.

"What did you find?" He urged me to continue.

"A monster..."

They each had a look of questioning at my revelation. I went on to describe the creature and what had happened in detail. Their faces grew more and more shocked by what I had found.

"I have no knowledge of what this beast could be," August informed me.

"It sounds more of a nightmare than reality," Ridge added.

"That was what I had thought, too. If I had not seen it with my own eyes, I would have difficulty believing in it, but it is real."

"We leave tomorrow. We can research this creature at the pack."

"I cannot leave my coven now. Not when they are in danger, just as you would not leave the pack if you thought something lurked our borders there."

They all nodded in understanding. With that sorted out, I needed to give them access to the coven.

"I need your hand," I held out my own to August.

I could tell he was uncomfortable, but he stretched his

out to mine. I held it as if it were a handshake and silently recited the spell that would allow them to pass.

"*Le m' thoil-sa bheir mi dhut dol a-steach dom fhearann.*"

Once it was completed, they would feel nothing more than a slight spark. I repeated the same actions with each of my pack members. My magic was still a new thing to them, so they looked over me with wonder and a bit of apprehension.

"You can now cross onto our land," I informed them.

"What did you do?" Ridge asked.

"I gave you permission," I smiled at them before stepping over to their Suburban and climbing in the front passenger seat. They all followed my lead, returning to the car. We made our way down the half-mile drive, pulling in next to Forest's car. The first hints of sunrise graced the sky as we unloaded. I led them through the empty grounds to my mother's house. It was the only home I knew had a place for them to sleep in.

As I approached the dark structure, a pang of sadness filled me. I had only flashes of memories with her since she died when I was three. I had always planned to move into the home when I had children of my own, but I mostly avoided it, not wanting to be reminded of my loss. The door was jammed from years of abandonment. August stepped up and used his shoulder to force the door open.

"It's a bit dusty here, but you will have it to yourselves. I will be at the large home we passed just down the trail. You can link me if you need anything."

I ensured they were settled and returned to the Nary house and my room. The welcomed security of my old quilt was desperately needed at that moment. The only thing that would have calmed me further was Forest, who was many miles away. Exhaustion finally took hold of my body and stole me to my dreams.

17

Forest

As I did every full moon, I approached my pack, which had gathered at the far end of Main Street. My large black paws pressed into the dusting of fresh snow that had fallen this morning. We gathered at the height of the moon, in the latest hour of the night. I pointed my head to the moon and let loose a deep and powerful howl. Each member of my pack joined in to create a harmonic symphony that echoed in the valley where our town had been built. As each voice slowly drew out, allowing the silence to take back control, I looked out across the crowd. A sea of natural colors moved before me, itching for my signal. There were several that were missing, one of which that I missed dearly, my mate.

My heart would break in two when she told me she was going to her coven for the full moon. Having her away from me, let alone unprotected, slowly ate away at my soul. The only way I could grant her wish was to send five of my men along with her. I would have preferred they stay with her at the settlement, ensuring her safety, but I knew the coven. It had been a trial just for myself, her mate, to join her on our past trips. They would never allow five unknown men onto their land. It would be too high of a risk.

I would have opted to go with her, but a lack of attendance on the full moon run would have significantly affected the pack. I was their leader, and I had to be there on the one night of the month we gathered together to celebrate our kind. The need was even more so due to the scents of rogues that had been picked up near our borders. After my mother was killed by one of those decrepit wolves, I vowed never to give them a chance again to take one of our people.

With the increasingly impatient crowd, I turned away from my pack and took off. The thundering sound of thousands of paws that followed me shook the ground beneath us. Even the thin layer of snow did nothing to soften the radiating waves of our force. We would follow the same track we did every full moon, heading north to the larger lake, following its shoreline made up of a series of angles and turns.

We crossed the river that fed the lake on the far north side and took to the hills. I looked up the mountain towards Juniper's glacial lake, which she could not stay away from, and wished that I could feel her presence there. I knew I would not find it, but it was just another reminder of the other half of my soul missing tonight. We were on the last portion of our run when I felt dread and fear clog my chest. I panted harder and looked around for any source of danger, finding none.

Do you sense anything? I asked Oakley.

Like what?

Danger...

I could see him out of the corner of my eye. He was a few paces back and to my left, the position of the beta.

He looked around our surroundings before replying, *No, I don't feel anything.*

My heart pounded in my chest, and I felt as if it were about to explode as this fearful feeling took hold of me. I could not figure out the source of my panic. I focused on my breath, willing it to even out. I cleared my mind, focusing only on this foreboding feeling. It was Juniper!

Juniper, I called out to her through our bond.

It should be impossible to feel her if she were at the coven, but I knew it was her. She must be close and in danger from this feeling.

Take the lead, I commanded Oakley.

What's happening? He asked, concerned, still looking for the danger around us.

Something's wrong with Juniper.

I pushed forward, letting my wolf run full speed, and I quickly pulled away from my pack. I raced through the empty streets and straight to the pack house. I could still feel her fear, unlike anything I had ever felt from her before. Even more so than when Sienna kidnapped her last summer. I needed to get to her. I grabbed a set of clothes in the front closet and ran to the garage down the street from the pack house. Opening a small cabinet, I grabbed the first set of keys, pressing the button to show me which car I had just claimed. One of the pack Suburban's lights flashed on the far side, and I ran over to start it up. The garage door barely opened before I sped out, tearing up the gravel leading back to the street. Without even a look back, I left our territory.

At the hour of the day I was traveling, the roads were empty, allowing me to fly down the highway. Juniper's fear eventually dissipated, but my worry about what had happened to her never lessened my urgency to get to her. The hours that it took to drive down felt unimaginably slow. I could feel her presence within the bond strengthening as I approached the small town near her coven. She was most definitely here, but what could have caused her to be so fearful?

As I approached the coven's gravel drive, the sun had not yet risen. I slowed down, unsure if I could pass their barrier without her. I was relieved when I found that I could do it without issue. I pulled into the parking area and saw my car and the pack Suburban there.

Juniper, I called out to her.

I could feel she was asleep, bringing me some peace. When she did not reply, I called for my gamma.

August, where are you?

Alpha, he replied, *slightly groggy. We are in one of the houses at the coven.*

Which one?

It is behind the Luna's house.

She must have put them in her mother's house. She had shown me where it was on one of our previous visits.

I will be there in a minute, I told him as I began to jog.

I followed the trail leading through the settlement, crossing the small wooden bridge. The snow was much deeper here, and I could see evidence of their recent activity left behind in its hold. I passed the Nary house, hearing the sound of people awake inside, and followed the tracks that led beyond it. August stood by the open doorway, lights flooding the night from within.

"Alpha," he bowed his head at me.

I walked past him and found all my men standing at attention inside.

"What happened?" I asked immediately.

"The Luna had an encounter with a creature in the woods. She called us here. We arrived just over an hour ago."

"What was the creature?"

"She described something that we do not know of, Alpha."

"It must have been something serious for me to feel her fear all the way to our pack."

They each looked stunned that that was even possible, as did I. But the fact that I was here, pulled by it, was evidence that it was true. They went on to fill me in on the story she had shared with them. Anger swelled inside me toward the creature that threatened my mate. I knew right then that I would hunt it down and kill it. No one, no thing, attacked my mate and survived.

"You all need rest," I told them as I returned to the door.

We would need all of our energy to kill this creature. I returned to the Nary house, quietly slipping in the front door. I could hear some rustling in the kitchen. I slipped off my untied boots and snuck up the stairs to Juniper's room, needing to get to my mate. I stood there, watching her sleep. Her face was locked in a grimace as she stirred. I stripped down, not wanting to bring my wet clothes into her warm bed, and pulled back the cover just enough to slip in. Her body instantly calmed, and she let out a small sigh as I wrapped my arms around her. She would always be safe with me.

18

Juniper

I felt warmth and comfort wrapped around me. It was as if I could still feel my dream of Forest, and I refused to wake any further, not wanting it to leave. I could even smell him here with me. I felt a stirring next to me and jumped up as my mind returned to the creature from the previous night. I flew out of my bed and screamed, but when I looked back, it was not the monster that haunted my mind but Forest.

"Forest? What? How? I mean, what are you doing here?" I stuttered out, trying to understand why he was standing before me.

My door flew open, and my Gran and Violet rushed into my room, stopping when they caught sight of my naked mate standing next to the bed. He grabbed my quilt and covered himself.

"What is going on here?" Violet asked angrily.

"I'm sorry, I was just startled."

Gran walked over to me and pulled me into her.

"Oh, sweet girl. No wonder you are a bit jumpy after what you have endured. Isn't that right, Violet?" she glared at her sister.

Violet pursed her lips as Gran turned her attention back to Forest, "Juniper had not told us you were in town. I'm surprised that you did not stay here with her."

"I only came this morning," he explained.

"I'm not surprised. It was quite the event last night," my Gran added.

"So I've heard," he grumbled.

Surprised, I looked over at him but realized that August must have called him.

"I'm sorry for waking you two," I told them.

"It's no problem at all, Juniper. We will let you two get dressed," Gran eyed Forest's body with a smirk. "I will fix you both some breakfast."

They closed the door as they left, and I hurried around my bed, wrapping myself around Forest's chest. Everything felt right as he held me. The fear from last night was instantly gone.

"Thank you for coming," I said into his chest.

"I will always come for you, Juniper."

We stayed wrapped around each other for several minutes before finally pulling back. I stood on my tiptoes and kissed him deeply.

When I returned to my feet, I looked back up at him and said, "We should go down for breakfast."

"Okay," he said, grabbing a pair of black sweatpants and a black t-shirt from the floor.

"Didn't you bring any clean clothes?" I asked him with a smile.

"No, I didn't take the time to grab anything. I can borrow something from August later."

I giggled as I grabbed some clothes from my bag. He walked over to the wooden chair in the corner of my room and picked up Ridge's shirt.

"Why is this here?" his jealousy peeking through.

I smiled at him, "Did you expect me to climb into the car with all the guys butt naked?"

He let out a low growl, "No..."

"I didn't think so."

"You could have driven."

"Forest, really? I went as my wolf."

He finally relented and paced the room while I dressed. We walked down the stairs to find everyone awake and at the long dining table. Either I slept in longer than I thought, or my scream had woken the whole house. Five Nary women lived in the main house, excluding myself. Once their daughters had their children, they usually moved back in, allowing the younger generations and their children to live on their own. Gran placed a bowl of scrambled eggs on the table alongside the toast and fruit.

"Alpha Forest, it's nice to see you," Fern, one of my aunts, said.

"It's nice to see you too. Thank you for having me."

"We hadn't realized you were one of the ones Juniper had asked to visit. You have an open invitation to join her when she comes."

"He only arrived this morning," Violet quipped.

"Oh," they all looked at him. "Well, it's so nice of you to come to her."

"Nothing could keep me away," he said, looking intently at me.

Fern and my cousin Jasmine giggled at his testament.

"How long has this creature been at your borders?" He questioned the table.

"Almost three weeks now," Jasmine answered.

"I would like to look around and see if we can find where it is hiding. Perhaps it has made a den close by."

"Absolutely not," Violet commanded, "Every time someone goes near it, it only worsens. I will not allow you to threaten our coven."

I could feel Forest's anger from being spoken down to. I reached under the table and held his leg, partly asking him not to snap back and to calm him.

"We will approach from the north. If it does spot us, we can draw it away."

"It's too dangerous," I objected as fear filled me.

"Six shifters versus one beast. I think the odds are in our favor," he reassured me.

"There are six of you?" Violet asked, still with a hint of entitlement in her voice.

I felt like she was grasping for control. She seemed to feel that Forest's presence challenged her position within the coven. He was a leader, the same as her, and she did not want him to be in charge.

"Yes, five of my men escorted Juniper down here," he explained to her, holding his composure.

"Were you worried we would hurt her?" Violet asked with disdain.

"No," he said bluntly, "but she is my mate, and it is a long drive. You should know how protective an alpha is of his mate."

There was a hint of warning in his voice. No one questioned him past that.

"We can bring it up in a meeting. I'm sure we need another after last night now that we have all had a chance to sleep on it," Gran suggested.

"Of course," Forest replied, his stern tone softening to her.

"Where are these friends of yours?" Fern asked.

"I put them in my mom's house," I answered her question.

"That was a good choice," Gran replied.

We finished breakfast, and then Forest and I walked over to see the others. I carried a basket with food Gran had made for them. I spread it out on the table, and they each instantly dove in.

"Thank you, Luna," they each said.

"Thank my Gran," I smiled back.

Forest leaned back against the kitchen counter and looked across the room at them.

"The coven is meeting this morning to decide if they want us to look into the creature."

"Why would they not want us to?" Ridge asked.

"The attacks against their ward have increased after they tried to investigate it themselves," I explained. "We should make a plan so that we can go as soon as it is approved."

I knew it took a hard toll on him not to be in charge, but he had previously worked with other alphas. The customs slightly differed, but they still required him to work diplomatically. I closed my eyes as I felt the ward's pressure push on my back, filling me with a sense of dread.

"What's happening, Juniper?" Forest asked me.

"It's back."

"How can you tell?" August asked.

"I can feel the ward being pushed. All of my coven can."

He nodded and looked back at Forest. I could tell he was

fighting the urge to race out and confront the creature here and now. I reached down and held his hand, calming him.

"The meeting should be starting soon. We should get going," I told them.

I led them to the center of the settlement. The women we passed leaned over to those next to them, whispering in their ears and giggling as if they were schoolgirls. When we entered the main hall, I had us stand at the back so as not to draw too much attention, though it helped very little.

Once everyone had arrived, Violet stood from the front table and said, "Sisters, today we are joined by members of the West Moon Pack."

All eyes turned to us.

Violet continued, "After last night's events, our visitors have offered to investigate the creature. I informed them that every interaction had only a negative effect on us. It was suggested that we bring it to a vote. So I ask you now. Sisters what say you on the matter of allowing the shifters to investigate further?"

"Before we begin," my Gran stood, interrupting the vote. "I believe that we should hear of their plans."

The sounds of agreement rolled across the room.

"Very well," Violet said. "Alpha Forest, please step forward so that you can inform us of your intentions."

Forest walked up to the front of the room, standing before the elders, "My men and I will circle outside the coven's land and approach the ward from the north. We will look for clues about where and if it has a den. We will lure it away from your borders and then kill it."

"Thank you, Alpha Forest," Violet said with a tinge of snark. "And so, sisters, what say you?"

Each person beside Violet raised their hand and stated their approval, passing the vote.

"When do you plan on enacting your plan, Alpha?"

"We will start the journey north now. Juniper can inform us when the beast is pushing on your ward. We will lure it away from there."

"Then go and find the monster," she said, gesturing to the door.

19

Forest

J uniper walked with us to the cars. We would shift and leave from there. A crowd was forming at the top of the trail. I suspected many curious eyes were there to watch the shifters change. We stood on the far side, allowing the cars to hide us. We did not shy from nudity but did not like to feel like we were on display, either.

"You guys can come through the ward at any point, so if you need a way to escape, use it," Juniper told us.

"We won't be needing it," I reassured her.

A single warrior could take on a grizzly alone. With six of us, including myself and my gamma, we would have no problem, even if it was a beast.

"Just remember it if you do," her voice was laced with concern.

I nodded to reassure her even though I doubted we would need to.

"We will head north and wait a few kilometers from your ward. When you feel it, link me," I told her.

"I will. Please be careful."

I smiled as I leaned down to kiss her, "I promise."

She stepped back, and I stripped down, handing her my clothes. The others followed suit, placing their clothes in the backseat of the car before we shifted. With one last look at Juniper, we took off down the drive. I could feel the eyes on me as we disappeared from view.

We crossed the main road, staying hidden on the other side. We crossed over again when it turned up the nearby mountain, staying outside the ward. They had said that the creature seemed to push in on the same spot, so we had a good idea of where to look. Juniper had shown me a map of the area and pointed out where she had seen it last night. It gave me a good idea of where to travel to get back there. I looked at the topography and noted certain features to use as landmarks. Using the mountain to our left, staying on track to our intended position was easy. We flew through the forest, giving a wide berth when we passed the mark where she had seen the creature.

Stay alert, I told the others.

We slowed, paying extra attention to our senses. I looked for any tracks the snow would reveal, but we found nothing besides the usual animal prints one would expect.

We will wait here for Juniper's call, I commanded.

Yes, Alpha, they each replied as they crouched into position.

We waited for hours, not catching any sign of it. As the sun teased the horizon, we heard a sound in the distance. It was still far away, but we could make out the heavy footfall of something making its way through the trees.

Be ready for the call, I redied them.

Shouldn't we go now while it's farther away? Ridge asked.

No. We do not want to scare it off if what we hear is just a bear. We need to confirm that the creature is attacking the coven.

Couldn't we sneak up on it to confirm?

Your Luna said that it has impeccable senses. If it could find her behind the ward, downwind, and with an invisibility spell, it would sense us before we could get close. If it is a bear, the creature would gain the upper hand against a surprise attack or flee away, and we would have to return later.

Yes, Alpha, he finally accepted.

Questioning could be a sign of distrust for their alpha, but I have always encouraged my men to do so. Doing so allowed them to learn and become better warriors. They needed to understand my tactics and the reasoning behind them so that they would make the same decisions as I would if I were not there.

The footsteps moved south right past the encounter site. The new ward was just over a kilometer and a half away. If it was, in fact, the beast, we should hear from Juniper soon. My wolf's urge to hunt fueled me with renewed energy as the anticipation grew. The others became restless as their primal needs swelled within them. Focusing on my senses in order for me to take in my surroundings, I could hear the last calls of songbirds in the distance, a snow hare leaping across the snow, and the trickle of water fighting for its freedom amongst the ice.

Forest, it's there, Juniper's voice rang through my head.

I leaped forward, chasing down the beast that hid amongst the trees—the one who tormented my mate. I had zero intention of letting it live past today. Our feet pounded through the thick snow, refusing to let it slow us in our mission. I was the first to spot the grotesque form. It whipped around and howled a haunting whistling sound into the wind before throwing its long arms out, revealing its devious claws. The smell of rotted flesh filled my nose, causing me to snarl.

It's sunken, evil eyes locked with mine as we came to a standoff. It only lasted a moment before the monster charged at me with a speed I had known no other to hold. A snarling whistle slipped past its rotten yellow fangs as it swung at me, nearly connecting. If I had not dodged at the last second, the battle may have ended at that moment for me. The others circled it, biting at the back of its mangy-furred legs.

As it swung for August's wolf, I prepared for another attack, pushing back on my hind legs and propelling myself towards it, aiming for the back of its neck. As if it anticipated my strike, it stopped mid-swing, redirecting it in my direction and slicing open my side. Pain rippled through my body, but I fought past it. I pulled myself up out of the blood-drenched snow just in time to see the beast uppercut my warrior Kai's face, sending him hurtling through the trees. I could hear his wolf whimper from the impact.

My anger fueled me to go after it again immediately. I charged at its legs, hoping to knock the beast down for the kill. But it was too fast. The monster twisted around quickly, hitting me with an unanticipated swipe of its massive arm and sending me flying into a nearby tree and falling, crumbling at its roots. I slowly pulled myself up but lacked the strength to avoid the beast's incoming strike that followed. I braced, preparing for the hit, when Ridge flew in front of me, taking the force of impact onto himself. He slammed into the ground, blood splattering across my face.

August and Denali bit at its legs, grabbing hold and tearing away the rotting flesh, baring its bones. I pulled myself up, feeling the damage done to my body. Its long arms had no problem reaching around and grabbing hold of them. August howled with pain as the dagger-like claws sliced through his body, and Danali whipped his head around, chewing at its hand. It tossed Denali through the trees; a loud thud informed me that he had impacted one hard. I growled loudly at it, pulling its attention away. It released August from its grasp, dropping him to the ground, and squared off with me.

Dylan, go for the back of the neck, I told my last standing warrior.

I watched the brown wolf circling behind it, preparing for his strike. I growled again, ensuring the monster's attention was on me. When it stepped towards me, I returned the charge, barely avoiding its claws and grabbing hold of its arm. At the same time, Dylan raced up, leaping from the snowy ground, and latched onto the back of its neck. It howled in pain as it reached over with its free hand, clawing into Dylan's back. He never let go of his hold as I ripped at the arm in my jaws, pulling a chunk of thick, meaty flesh with me. I dropped to the ground and lunged for the other arm. It was too quick, removing it from Dylan's body and back, handing me across the small clearing.

I heard a whimper from Dylan and watched the blood pour down his body, soaking the earth beneath him. He did not have much left in him. I tried to stand, but my blood loss had made me weak, and I collapsed back to the ground. Dylan fell from its back, landing limp on its jaggedly clawed feet. It turned and looked at his body, reaching down and grabbing hold of his limp form, then hoisted it up to its mouth and took a bite from his neck. I could feel his bond to the pack sever as he died at the hands of the creature.

I could not let this thing go. I tried once more to lift myself from the ground. The sound of the snow compressing below me drew its attention, and it dropped

Dylan's lifeless body back to the bloody ground before turning to me. I growled at it, not willing to submit to my fate. Its horrid visage slowly stalked towards me, and I prepared for the end.

Suddenly, a massive fireball flew through the trees, striking it on its back. Its fur burst into flames, and it wailed to the heavens with its whistling voice as it swiped at its back with its hands. Another ball came hurtling from the forest, striking it once more. The monster looked towards the source, as did I. Juniper stood squarely opposed to it. Her bare body contrasted against the stark white surroundings. It began to charge at her, flames flowing from its skin.

No, I yelled, worried that it would go after her.

I mustered everything I had left to chase after it, refusing to allow it to hurt my mate, my Juniper. She pulled her hands to her chest, breathing deeply. A flame came to life, floating within her hands. It proliferated until it had filled her grasp, and she hurtled it at the creature, hitting it square in the face. It stumbled and fell backward with another eerie howl, then fell silent, lying still in the snow. I froze, waiting to see if she had defeated the beast, but my hope was short-lived. Its arm lifted, pushing against the ground, raising itself to its towering height. I prepared to keep going, refusing to allow it to attack my mate, when it screamed at her in a shriveled voice reminiscent of an old woman before it turned in the opposite direction and fled back into the blackened forest. Juniper ran towards me. She dropped to her knees and held my battered body against her own.

"Forest, oh Goddess..." she looked me over with concern. "I could feel you."

My wolf whimpered as we finally took notice of the severity of our injuries.

"We need to get out of here. I don't know if it will return," she said fearfully.

She looked back at the others and brought her hands to her mouth in shock. She stood and raced over to August and inspected his injuries.

"He's still alive! We need to get them back to the coven," I groaned to her.

We heard a sound coming from the trees behind her. We both jumped, fearing the beast's return, but sighed in relief when Kai limped out from the brush. His face was mangled, with blood still dripping from his snout. Juniper rushed to him, carefully running her fingers across his shredded face.

"Kai, can you help us?" she asked him softly.

Y-yes, Luna, he linked back weakly.

Though it would be easier to carry the others out in our human forms, we would heal faster like this. I walked over to August, who was lying unconscious in the snow, and grabbed ahold of his scruff as I began dragging him toward the coven. Kai grabbed Ridge while Denali, who had limped out from the undergrowth, followed our lead and grabbed hold of Dylan's scruff. Juniper led us as we pulled our injured across the rough terrain and deep snowpack to the safety of her coven. I felt it when we crossed the ward nearby, which gave us some semblance of safety. By the time we reached the meadow, the other coven members had come to meet us. They must have followed Juniper when she came to our aid. They made quick work fashioning sleds to pull us back to the settlement. When they offered one to me, I refused.

Please, Forest. You are bleeding. Let us take care of you, Juniper begged me.

With the fear in her heart, I relented, laying myself on

the sled made of branches and the coven sister's coats. They began to pull me and the others back to their home.

20

Juniper

When I felt the first stab of pain through our bond, I dropped to the ground. The pain radiated from my side.

"What's wrong, Juniper?" my Gran asked, concerned, as she helped me up.

I panted as I focused on Forest.

"He's injured. I have to go to him," I said, fearing for my mate.

"It's too unsafe, Juniper," she pleaded with me as I pulled myself up.

"I don't care. They need me," I shouted as I ran through the door, shifting as soon as I cleared its frame.

My clothes tore away from my body as it transformed. I spotted the others watching me as I raced through the settlement. I focused on Forest, taking a deep breath. I could see the monster coming after them in my imagination. They were too far away for me to reach them quickly, so I did the only thing I could think of: I prayed to Selene for help. As I asked for her help, I began to recite a spell, one that I had not known before. Nor did I know where it came from.

"*Selene, mas e do thoil e, Thoir dhomh astar na gaoithe*"

I felt a whoosh of wind whip from behind me, propelling me through the woods. My legs still touched the earth, but I moved faster than ever as if the wind carried me. I could hear the battle ahead. I came to a halt as I watched the monster bite into Dylan, his light leaving him. A familiar growl came from the opposite side of them. The creature dropped Dylan's body and turned. My eyes looked to where it faced, finding Forest injured and surrounded by blood-soaked snow. My stomach twisted, and my breath caught in my throat as I saw my strong and powerful mate so vulnerable. The beast stepped towards him. Panic filled me, and I shifted back, intending to scream to draw it away from him. I was still behind the ward. I hoped that it would slow it enough to allow Forest to escape.

Fire, a voice said in my mind.

I did not have time to think about who or what it was; I simply followed its instructions. I had never been good at fire spells, but perhaps I could distract it. I cupped my hands together at my chest.

"*Sradag na beatha, sradag solais. Lìon mo làmhan le cumhachd teine.*" I whispered.

I could feel the warmth grow within my hands. I looked down, surprised to find a ball of flames swirling around in my grasp. I did not waste a moment and threw it towards the monster. A whistling scream escaped the beast as the fire engulfed its furry back. As quickly as I had made the first, I created a second, throwing it once more. It turned and faced me. I could sense its rage as it began to charge at me. My heart thundered as I threw another sphere of fire at it, connecting with its face. It dropped to the ground, and I held my breath, preparing to make another fireball. When it stood, I began to recite the words, but it turned and ran away before I could send another volley.

I HELPED the others bring Forest and my other pack members into the main hall. My coven sisters instantly went to work, tending to their wounds. A white wool blanket was placed over Dylan's body, cementing his death in my mind. It was hard to accept it. After the pack's wounds had been treated, the others left, leaving only the elders, my Gran, and myself. My Gran led me to the elders who whispered away in the corner.

"Juniper, we are sorry for your loss," Pearl told me as she grasped my hands.

A tear dropped from my eye.

"Four of them will survive. Their injuries are already healing," Violet said somberly. "The one on the end, however, has grave injuries. We can do no more to help him. It is now up to Selene."

I looked over at August's still body.

"There has to be something?" I pleaded.

"I am sorry, Juniper," Violet replied.

I could not accept their answer.

"W-what about the moon spell? The one to give him Selene's power pulled in from the moon."

"Beatha gealaich," my Gran thought aloud.

"Yes, that one." I turned to face them, a small hope beginning to burn inside me.

"Juniper, that spell is old. It has not been performed in generations," Violet told me.

"No, I have done it before."

"When?" Violet asked, surprised.

Violet knew of the possibility of me wielding strong power due to her grandmother, Iris, being born of a shifter father. I had never shared with anyone beyond my Gran the spells I had been able to cast during the events surrounding Sienna or my commune with Selene.

"The first time I cast it was not long after I arrived at the pack. There was an explosion that gravely injured a man," I told them.

"You have completed the spell more than once?" She further questioned.

"Yes, the second was on myself."

I could see the stunned faces amongst them.

"That has only been performed by the most powerful of witches," Pearl spoke in disbelief.

"Juniper wields a strong amount of power," Gran added.

She obviously had not shared my conversation with the elders with Selene all those months ago.

"If this is true, then we shall let her try," Violet proposed.

The way she spoke, it felt like she intended it to be some form of test, but if it saved August's life, it didn't matter. The materials were quickly gathered. We pulled August back onto one of the makeshift sleds. I heard the crack of the bone as Forest shifted and started to get up.

"Stop, Forest, you need to rest," I ran over to him, touching his shoulder.

"I'm fine, Juniper. I can already feel myself healing," he grumbled, his pain still evident.

"I know, but there is nothing you can do right now," I reassured him.

"I can help you carry him," he said adamantly.

"You are still too injured. It could reopen your wounds," I told him softly.

He sighed, "At least let me come with. He is my Gamma and friend."

I looked back at the others who left their words unsaid.

"Fine," I helped him up and put his arm over my shoulder.

One of the elders brought him a blanket that he draped over himself, and I supported him as we walked out. The elders and my Gran managed to pull August out without me. Even in their old age, they were still strong.

The moon was high in the sky, as night had long since taken over. Gran placed a bowl of water above August's head and then handed me a rough moonstone. I put it on his still fur-covered chest, resting my hand over it. Raising my free hand to the moon, I blew a deep, long breath over his body.

"Selene, mo mhàthair. Thoir dhomh do sholas gus an urrainn dhomh beatha a thoirt air ais don leanabh agad. Cleachd mi mar do làmhan, do shùilean agus do bhodhaig. Thoir do thiodhlacan don leanabh agad. Is leatsa mo chorp-sa airson a chleachdadh airson do ghnìomh," I chanted five time.

Each time, I felt the moon's energy flow through my body and into his. Unlike the first time I cast the spell, I did not succumb to exhaustion. I could still feel the effects but push past the wariness and stay conscious. I sat back on the cold ground. The dampness from the earth seeped through the dress Gran had fetched me. I swayed side to side, feeling depleted. We listened as August's ragged breaths began to even out, and his heart sped up, leveling at his regular rate. Violet stepped up to him and peeled back his bandages.

"Look," Pearl gasped, pointing to his injuries.

I watched before my eyes as they stitched themselves

back together. Shifters had a rapid healing ability, but even this was unbelievable. It reminded me of myself after I had been stabbed. I had not watched it happen, but I felt my body healing itself.

August's wolf let out a sigh as his bones began cracking. The fur that covered his body receded into his skin. His paws grew fingers and toes. His shift was slow, but it was happening. Once complete, he opened his eyes and looked around.

"What's going on here?" he asked nervously, looking around the gathered women.

"August!" Forest called from the side.

"Alpha, you're hurt!" August said quickly as he jumped up and raced over to him.

"I will be fine." He looked him over, "and it appears you will too."

August looked down at his body, finding only dried blood stuck to his skin.

"What happened?" he questioned.

He looked over at me, realization spreading across his face, "Did you?"

I smiled weakly at him.

"Luna, you're awake?" he said, surprised.

"I guess I'm getting better at it."

He stood taller and bowed his head to me, "I am eternally grateful to you, Luna."

I could only smile again as speaking had become too taxing on my depleted body. Forest walked over and handed August the blanket wrapped around him.

"You may need this," he said wryly.

Forest then walked over to me, bending down and lifting me into his arms bridal style.

"Forest, no. You're still too weak," I croaked out.

"It's my turn to care for you, my love."

Without another word to anyone else, he carried me away to my family's home, where we would hide away in my bed, tangled within each other's arms all night.

21

Juniper

I watched Forest talk on the phone and listened to his conversation.

"Let me get this straight, Alpha. You and the others were attacked, and Dylan is dead?" Oakley's voice spoke through the phone in disbelief.

"You heard me right; I want twenty warriors down here today. There is a beast in these woods, and it will not live through tomorrow."

"Yes, Alpha."

I could tell that Oakley hated having to stay back at the pack, but one of the high-ranked wolves had to be present at all times to protect and lead everyone. Forest hung up the phone and looked back at me.

"Have you felt it push the ward anymore since yesterday?" he asked.

"No."

"It could be healing. We cannot let it get away and terrorize someone else."

I dropped my head slightly, "I know."

I understood and agreed with him, but I had been so close to losing him last night. I was scared for him to go after it again.

He walked over and caressed my cheek, "I'm going to check on the others."

"Okay, I am supposed to meet with the elders," I told him.

"Do you want me to come with you?" he asked.

I shook my head, "No, I need to do this alone."

He leaned into me and kissed my forehead, "Link me if you change your mind."

"I will."

He darted off through the door. The others' injuries had mostly healed throughout the night, allowing them to return to my mother's house. Ridge had taken a brutal hit to the head and was slashed across his chest. He was fortunate that it only punctured his lung rather than his heart. Kai's face mainly had healed up. Fortunately, the only way shifters scarred is if wolfsbane or silver were used, meaning he would have no traces left of the mangled features from the fight. I grabbed my coat from the hook near the door and pulled it on tightly before heading out.

"Hey," Meadow said as she walked through the gate leading up to the Nary house.

"Hey, what are you up to?"

"I came to check on you. That was insane last night," she gawked at me wide-eyed.

I let out a long breath, "It was."

"How is everyone doing? I heard someone died," her voice turned nervous.

Sadness crept back into me.

"His name was Dylan..." I whispered.

She looked down at the ground and pushed the snow with the toe of her boot. It was hard to comprehend how it had happened so fast. Everyone, even myself, had clearly underestimated this creature.

"So this thing, it's really bad?" She asked hesitantly.

"Yeah. It took them all down. I was lucky to get there in time to help."

"What's going to happen now?"

"I will ask the elders if more pack members can come down. Forest is determined to go back out after it."

"After it nearly killed him?" she said, raising her voice in shock.

"That's shifters for you," I shrugged, trying to hide my fear.

"They're crazy," she huffed.

"They're determined. Hunting and territorial dominance are ingrained in them. Not only has the creature stirred their primal instincts, but after it killed one of our own, they feel the need to avenge him."

"Are you like that now?"

"Kind of. When I am in my wolf form, I feel the urge to hunt. I have caught a few rabbits here and there, and once, Forest and I took down a deer. It's weird, though. It's like my wolf takes over for that part. I'm just a passenger along for the ride. It's nothing more than the traps we set in the woods."

The coven also promoted the balance of nature. We ate meat and vegetables, but we only took what we needed. We never waste any part of an animal, always using all of its bones, furs, and meat.

"Anyway," I said, "Thanks for checking in on me. I have to go meet with the elders."

"Good luck," she said, contorting her face with unease.

I laughed, "Thanks, you know I'll need it."

"Yes, you will." She replied as she went into the house.

As I walked down the trail, an intense pressure pushed on me. I stopped, frozen in my tracks, and looked north. The creature had already returned. I had hoped that it would hide away after it ran off yesterday and heal for at least a few days. Maybe it would have even been completely scared away from our border, but we had no such luck. It felt more substantial than before, as if it was more determined now, like it was fighting the ward even harder. At this rate, I didn't know how much longer it would hold.

Are you alright, Juniper? Forest linked me, sensing the pit of fearfulness that pulled at my insides.

He was checking on me as he did every time my nerves flared.

It's back, I whispered to him as I accepted the situation.

Already?

Yes. It feels determined, I told him.

Fuck, okay. I will let the others know.

I entered through the heavy wooden double doors of the main hall. Sunlight flooded through the space from the large circular windows on either end, highlighting the wooden floors and walls. The table where the elders typically sat was surrounded by chairs; rather than lined up on one side, the six women were already seated.

"Please take a seat, Juniper," Violet called across the vast room.

My footsteps echoed off the walls as I crossed the space, pulling off my coat before sitting at the elder's table. I looked across their faces, unable to read their expressions, which twisted my stomach slightly.

"Thank you for joining us. Our intention with this meeting is to discuss your power," Violet announced.

I was slightly shocked. When they sent word that morning, I had assumed they wanted to talk about the creature and the events of last night.

"What about my powers?" I questioned.

"Last night, you were able to cast one of our most powerful spells—one that has not been performed in generations. While we have not had a use for the spell over the last few decades, it is still known as powerful magic usually only cast by the strongest of our coven. Since you have successfully completed the spell three times, we need to investigate your powers."

Investigate my powers? Were they concerned that I had done the spell? As far as I knew, it was not a banished spell.

Violet said, "As you know, a witch's power grows with her lifespan. It is one of the reasons elders, such as us, lead the coven. We want to ask you what spells you have accomplished so far."

"Um, okay. Like what?" I asked hesitantly.

"Any powerful spell that you have successfully cast."

"Well, you know of the one from last night. Yesterday, with the creature, I could throw a fireball."

"A fireball?" Briar, the elder from the Kelly family, asked with equal parts shock and questioning.

"Describe this fireball, as you call it," Violet requested.

"It was larger than a softball. I created it with my hands and could throw it at the creature."

"That is fascinating," the Martin elder replied.

Up until yesterday, I had no idea that something like that could have been cast. We could make fire, which we used to light candles and fires in our hearths, and we could even hold a small flame in our hand, but the amount of energy that creating an actual fireball that could be thrown would take was unimaginable. I was still shocked that I had been capable of such a thing, and from the elders' reactions, it seemed they were equally as stunned.

"How did you come up with the idea to create it?" Violet further questioned.

"Honestly, when I arrived, all I could think about was fire. It was like it...just came to me."

Violet hummed, "Have there been any other strong spells besides the two?"

"About six months ago, I was able to absorb an explosion. I pulled the energy into my hands and extinguished it. I don't even remember how I did it. I had just performed the, what did my Gran call it? Beatha gealaich spell? I had cast the spell on myself, having been injured when the explosion happened. Time moved so fast, yet so slow at the same time. The words just came to me."

Pearl raised her hands, "Great Selene, I am honored to be in front of your chosen one."

"Chosen, what?" I asked, startled. "I'm not a chosen one."

"Your powers are above all others, and yet you are still so young," she said, looking at me with adoring eyes.

"I think it is just my two halves coming together. Two sides of her power," I countered.

"There is something more to you," Violet said, looking me over.

I could not quite tell if it was suspicion or intrigue.

"I don't know what you're talking about. I'm just me. There is nothing special about me. I guess, except that I have shifter blood."

"We will have to see," Violet replied, resting her chin on the back of her hand.

"I, um, I thought that you wanted to discuss the creature."

"There is nothing to discuss," Violet replied, waving off my comment.

"How is there nothing to discuss? It nearly wiped out six shifters and succeeded in killing one."

"Exactly, they were of no help. If anything, they only angered it further. We will go back to our original plan and wait it out. It will eventually grow tired and leave us."

"You can't know that. If whatever that thing is gets past the wards, it will slaughter you! All of you."

"We are not without our power, Juniper," Violet challenged me. "We will be prepared if it does."

"What with? Compared to shifters, we are gravely under-prepared. Most women here know how to send wind, start small fires, and put up a shield, but we are not aggressive enough to take it on. Even if you find a way to defeat it, there will surely be casualties. Would you not rather be rid of it now while you are protected behind the wards?"

"This is not up for discussion," she stated sternly.

"More shifters can come down, a lot more. They can take it out now. We can work with them. We can stop it before it hurts someone."

"I have already told you that this is not up for discussion," she seethed at my persistence.

"At least let the coven vote on it," I begged.

"No," she glared at me, "We will not allow more of those men, those shifters, to invade our coven."

"I am a shifter!" I yelled at her.

"And we can see where your loyalty lies. Perhaps it is time for you and your kind to leave."

I was shocked. She couldn't kick me out of my own coven. Even Violet did not hold that type of authority.

"Perhaps we should take some time to cool off," Pearl

interjected softly, looking back and forth at us. Juniper, why don't you go for now, and we can meet again later?"

"There will be no other meeting," Violet stood her ground.

"We will see about that," I said before storming away.

What's wrong? Forest linked me.

He could feel the rage that burned within me.

My Aunt Violet is a little too full of herself right now.

Do you need me?

No, I took a deep breath. *I'm on my way to you.*

I pulled on my jacket and ran my hands down my face. The elders led our coven, but decisions were made collectively. Violet had overstepped her role. She could not solely dictate what happened. I would not let her endanger my family due to her stubborn and arrogant ways.

I entered my mother's cabin and found the others seated around the dining table. I was sure my expression gave away my sour mood. All but Forest bowed their heads and greeted me while Forest stood and pulled me into his chest.

"They won't let the pack onto coven lands," I told him.

"Why?" he asked, pulling me back so that he could see my face.

"Violet has this grandiose delusion that the creature will eventually leave on its own, and she doesn't want any more outsiders on our land."

"I can have them stay in town until we can get this sorted," he offered.

"Thank you," I told him, feeling slightly relieved.

At least I knew Forest took this situation as seriously as I did.

"Is there anything we can do to convince them to accept our help?" August asked.

I sighed, "Violet is as stubborn as a mule. There is no

convincing that woman once her mind is made up, however..." I stated as a thought popped into my mind, "I could try and get the rest of the coven on board. She would have no choice but to accept it then."

"Looks like you have some work to do then?" Forest smiled at my determination.

I bit my lip, "I guess I do."

22

Juniper

"They would only be here for protection and to help get rid of the beast," I told Elder Pearl as I sat at her dining room table. Once the creature was gone, then they would leave, too."

"We have never opened the gates for outsiders before. I worry that they will be hard to close again once they are open."

"You have allowed Forest and the others to stay. The gates are already open, and all they are trying to do is to help us."

"I know, Juniper. People fear the unknown, and your pack is, well...unknown."

"I'm not. I trust these men with my life. Can't you trust me?"

"I wish it were that simple. Even if we were to remove the spell allowing them entry, they could share our existence with others."

"The pack already knows the coven is here."

"They don't know our exact location...right?"

"No, but they know it's somewhere in North-central Washington."

"That is a lot of land for them to cover in search of us. We are well hidden for a reason."

"I know why we stay hidden. After our ancestors were chased out of Scotland, the surviving members did what they had to. Times have changed. I am not asking us to go public to the world, to the humans. I am just asking the coven to accept help to survive."

The threatening pressure of the creature's return to our ward pushed on me once more. Pearl and I stared at the wall, waiting for it to leave. She looked back at me with fear in her eyes.

"Perhaps it is time for us to change."

"Thank you, Pearl," I said, holding her hand.

As I walked down the trail to the next home, the ward pushed on me once more. It had only been ten or so minutes since it had happened last. The creature was becoming more persistent. I climbed up the pathway when I was suddenly pushed to the snowy ground by an immense force. Dazed and confused, I sat up, quickly realizing what had just happened. Our outermost ward had broken. The beast had broken through. I jumped to my feet and began racing to the main hall.

Forest, the creature, has broken the ward. I'm going to the main hall. Meet me there, I linked him as I ran.

We're on our way, he replied quickly.

I saw others running as well, some without jackets or boots. It was an alarming moment that none of us would waste time reacting to. If it broke through one, there would be no stopping it from eventually passing through another.

I joined the others who pushed through the doorway

and filed into the room. I could hear crying and worry amongst the crowd. I fought through the swarmed mass of women and looked around for my Gran. I had been on the far side of the settlement when the ward broke. She would have had plenty of time to arrive. Panic began filling me until I saw her entering the hall out of the corner of my eye.

"Gran!" I called as I made my way back to her.

"Juniper," she said, relieved. "Are you alright, my child?"

"I'm fine? Are you?"

"I'm just fine," she said, squeezing my hand.

Forest and the others entered, and I rushed into his arms. I had no time to talk to him before Violet stood and began to hush the crowd.

"Sisters, we cannot panic. The creature is still outside two wards. Let us calm ourselves so that we can think clearly."

As everyone settled, she stepped in front of the table.

"Our plans have not changed. We will continue practicing our defensive spells. If the creature makes it past the last of our wards, we will be prepared."

"What if it kills someone?" Someone shouted from the other side of the room.

"We will not allow that to happen."

"It has already killed one of the shifters. What is it to stop it from killing us?" another woman cried out. "We have not trained for something like this."

"We are training now," Violet replied sternly.

I could sense the fear within the room. No one believed we would survive. Our people were peaceful. While our elders wielded more power, we practiced simple spells. We could create fire, wind, and direct water, but not at the level required to defeat this creature. Even with the use of my invisibility spell, it had sensed me. Without help, the coven would be all but defenseless. I knew that I had to do something.

"Allow more shifters to enter our lands," I called across the room. "Allow them to help protect us."

"No," Violet shouted angrily. "This topic has already been closed, Juniper Nary. You dare go against your elders' ruling?"

"If I must in order to protect the coven, then yes," I said confidently.

"I, Violet Nary, ban you from our hall," she spoke through her teeth, rage burning in her eyes.

"You cannot do that without the full vote of the elders. You are not our leader, but one of six," I challenged her. "I look to you now, elders of the Whispering Creek Coven. Do you wish to fight this battle alone, or would you accept help so as not to die?"

The room was as silent as a cold winter's night. Only the slight whistling of the breeze slipping through a crack could be heard. The elders looked at each other, but I only watched Violet's raging face staring back at mine.

Pearl stood from her chair. "What say you sisters? Shall we allow warriors from the West Moon Pack to come upon our land to aid in our fight with this creature? After the creature has been defeated, the warriors shall leave our land and not return unless otherwise invited?"

"I have not given my approval," Violet turned to Pearl, her building anger surfacing.

"To put it to a vote within the coven, we only need the majority of the elders to approve. We do not require your agreement, Violet," she said cautiously.

"What say thee, sisters?" Pearl spoke to the room again.

A nearly unanimous aye echoed through the room.

"All those opposed?"

Violet, once more, was one of very few whose voices sang out against my proposition.

"So it shall be. Alpha Forest Juniper will assist you in allowing your men entry. We shall work on accommodations for them."

"Thank you," he replied, "They can stay at Juniper's mother's home if she allows. We do not require much."

Pearl nodded at him before redirecting her attention to the rest of the coven.

"In the meantime, be prepared. We shall continue practicing our spells. Little ones should be kept indoors. All chores that are not essential will be postponed until further notice. If the next ward brakes, we shall shelter here in the hall."

With Pearl's direction, a sliver of ease began to break the hold of fear that had taken root. Slowly, the others began to filter outside. Those without shoes and jackets waited so that others could retrieve the items for them. I walked with Forest back up to the Nary household to call Cole, who was leading the warriors down to us.

We slipped off our jackets and boots and walked through the main sitting room to our landline. Our coven's remoteness meant there was no signal for our cell phones to work. While I had brought mine, its only purpose was for emergencies and communication on the journey to and from the coven. Forest picked up the phone and dialed Cole's number. It rang only once before it was answered.

"Hello?" Cole's voice came through.

"Cole, you and the others will come to the coven. Link me when you are near, and I will meet you on the main road near the coven's drive.

"Yes, Alpha."

The front door opened, and Violet stepped in. I had not

expected her back so quickly. She marched across the room to me. Forest's arm wrapped around my waist, pulling me to his side, keeping himself between the two of us. She stopped and stared at us.

"You and your wolves are going to be the downfall of our coven."

I bit the inside of my cheek to not lash out at her. Arguing would serve no purpose in this situation, and the lack of a response only angered her more. She turned and went straight to the stairs, glaring back at us again before ascending. Forest finished telling Cole the directions to the coven and hung up.

"Is she going to be a problem?" he asked with a slight growl.

I looked back at the stairs, asking the same question.

"No...she's just angry. She wouldn't do anything to harm the coven," I reassured him, though I was not convinced.

"What about harming you?" he asked, staring intently at me.

I looked up at him, mixed emotions flitting across my face. "I don't think so," I said.

"You should stay with us at your mother's home."

I sighed, knowing that he was right. Even though I did not think Violet would ever do anything to me, I did not want to spend my time with her in the house.

"Okay," I agreed.

My Gran, who had stayed back to help some of the others, came in through the door as we came down the stairs with my bag in hand.

"Where are you going?" she asked worriedly.

"I think it is better for me to give Violet some space," I told her.

"Nonsense," she said sternly. "That sister of mine

needed to be knocked down a peg. You did the right thing. She will come to see that as well, in time."

"Well, I think I will give her that time without Forest and me rooming across the hall from her."

My Gran pursed her lips slightly," If that is what you want."

"It is," I assured her.

"Do you have everything you need? Bedding, towels?"

"I already brought some over for them this morning," I told her.

"Alright then, my dear. I expect to see you both for meals."

"We'll try," I smiled at her as we hugged.

Forest helped me put on my jacket, and we left. The house was only a five-minute walk from the Nary house, but as night settled, the trail was dark. An incoming storm was sending an icy breeze through the darkened forest. The whistling sound it made sent shivers down my spine, reminding me of what lurked within. We dropped my bag off before heading back out to meet the incoming warriors.

By the time we arrived, they were already waiting at the coven's drive. Three black SUVs that matched the others parked at the coven lined the side of the narrow road. Cole stepped out and bowed his head to us.

"All the warriors need to step out to gain entry," Forest directed.

The doors flew open, and the warriors filed out in front of us, one after the other. Forest looked at me, waiting for me to begin.

"My coven has never let outsiders in before. I ask that you respect their boundaries. Do not wander unless invited. These women are sheltered; many have never met a man before."

"Yes, Luna," they each said in chorus.

I stepped up to the first, taking his hand in mine. I whispered the words, allowing him entry before moving on to the next. I watched as the others eyed me with the same look of bewilderment August and the original group had shown when I had cast the same spell on them. Once I had enchanted all twenty of our warriors, I stepped back to Forest's side.

"Three of you will drive the cars in; the rest will follow us," he told them.

Whenever he spoke to his warriors, I felt his alpha aura radiating off him like a thick blanket of power. We walked down the half-mile drive, the cars slowly following behind us. None of my coven sisters were out. I suspected that they all hid in their homes, still feeling the emotions of the day. I spotted a few faces in the windows as we passed them. Curious eyes wanted to spot the small army of men that followed me.

Once inside my mother's home, we gathered in the small living room. Forest began to brief his warriors on the situation and start laying out the foundations of a plan.

"Tomorrow at dusk, we will split into three groups. I will lead the first group North like we traveled the other night. Group two will be led by August and will cover the coven's northern border inside their ward."

He looked at me and said, "Can you take them out tomorrow to show them where the outermost ward is located?"

"Yes."

He returned his focus to the group in front of us.

"Group three will be led by Cole. He and his men will stay within the second and final ward that they have put into place surrounding the settlement. Your group shall be small but necessary to protect the women of the coven. If the creature is able to slip past us, it will be up to you to protect them."

"Juniper, is there a way to strengthen the ward?" He asked me.

"Only with us being there. When we set a ward, the elders travel the perimeter of where they want it and cast the spell as they walk. In order to strengthen it, I suppose we would need witches every hundred feet or so."

"Would they be willing to do that?" he asked further.

"I can ask, but I would be surprised if they agreed. Everyone has become scared to travel out of the settlement."

He nodded at me and then turned his focus back to his men.

"My group will wait for the signal either from your Luna or from group two regarding the creature's location. This thing has long claws and arms, giving it a deadly reach. We must work together to bring it down. Tomorrow, we will train at dawn."

A unified chorus acknowledged his words before the men dispersed. A knock came at the door, and everyone stilled. I walked over, laughing inside at how on guard each of them was, though the more I thought about it, the more it made sense. They were in unknown territory and knew that they were not exactly welcome. I pulled open the door to find my Gran and Meadow with their arms full of dishes and food. Both of their eyes racked over the towering men behind me. I could tell Meadow was biting her tongue to keep her comments in check.

"We thought your pack members would be hungry after their travels," Gran said, stepping in without hesitation.

"Thank you, Gran," I smiled warmly at her.

Several men stepped forward, taking the hot food from her, and carried it to the kitchen.

"Would you like to come in and join?" I asked her.

"Uh, yeah. I can't miss out on this." Meadow said in her drooling tone.

Gran pushed her shoulder with her own. A clear sign that she expected her to behave herself.

"That would be lovely, my dear." She said, stepping into the crowded room.

We enjoyed Gran's Forest Stew and fresh-baked bread. Meadow never stopped gawking at the warriors, but my Gran seemed at ease amongst them. She listened to their stories of pack life and warrior training. It was a nice distraction from tomorrow's impending battle—one that we all needed.

23

Juniper

I shot straight up out of my slumber, gasping for breath. "What's wrong?" Forest asked, concerned, as he sat up and held me.

"The ward!" I breathed out, "the creature..."

I could still feel it. It was learning how to push through. No longer did I feel light pressure, but it was an over-whelming force. I closed my eyes to focus further on it, wishing I could see what it was doing.

"It's moving..."

"What do you mean?"

"It's not coming from the north this time."

"Where is it coming from?"

"It's moving East."

Forest let out a deep sigh. If the creature moved, their plan would be more difficult. They would not know where to lay in wait for it, possibly ending up in its path.

"Let me know if you continue to feel it move around."

"I will."

With the pressure decreasing, I laid back down with Forest. The sky was still dark outside of the two small windows. We lay in what used to be my mother's room. Her full-sized bed was small to fit Forest's large frame and my own body, but we didn't mind being wrapped around one another. The others had all found spots on the floor. Nearly every square inch was covered by the twenty-four men who slept on it. August had taken my old twin bed in the second bedroom. Again, its tiny frame was dwarfed by his size.

I rolled onto my side so that I could look at Forest.

"We're going to be fine, right?"

He rolled to face me and pushed a stray hair behind my ear.

"We will. I will never let anything happen to you."

"What about you? Nothing can happen to you either."

"There are many more of us this time. We will defeat it."

I tucked my head under his chin. Forest's lack of fear comforted me. I could feel nothing but love from him. He kissed the top of my head before wrapping his arms around me and sliding them down my waist. It had been so long since we had the opportunity to be together. Between my being gone and the crowdedness of each home we slept in, the opportunity had yet to present itself. All I wanted was to climb on top of him and ride him until the rest of the world disappeared, but with men asleep right outside our door, that was not possible. Forest had other ideas as his hand slipped into my pajama pants, cupping my ass.

"What are you doing? There are too many people here."

"Not if we stay quiet," he grinned at me mischievously.

He leaned down and sucked on the side of my neck, pulling a moan from me.

"F-forest," I fought through my uncontrollable need for him.

His hands slid across my skin, igniting sparks inside of my body. I felt my pajama bottoms pulled down, and I lifted my hips, allowing the warm fabric to slip past my thighs. The fight in me quickly dissipated, and I caved into my primal need: to be with my mate.

Our mouths came together as he climbed on top of me. His fingers played with me, swirling across my clit before pushing within me. I rolled my head back, taking a deep breath in. His mouth returned to my neck, his tongue gliding down the front of my throat. My hands held his muscular arms tightly as I anchored myself. My breathing became heavy, and I buried my face into his shoulder to muffle any noises that might escape me. When I began to peak, I bit down into his shoulder so that I did not scream out with pleasure.

He licked his fingers clean before slipping inside of me. I let out a gasp at the welcomed intrusion. Wrapping my legs around his waist, I pulled him deeper and matched his thrusting with my own rhythmic movements. Our bodies moved as one as we made passionate love to each other.

With the first sign of day creeping through the curtains, we untangled our bodies and slipped out of bed. I pulled my mother's old robe on and tied it around my waist, planning to sneak down the hallway to the lone bathroom in the house. When I peeked out the door, I was surprised to see the hallway that had been filled by sleeping men last night already empty. I had hoped that they had not heard Forest and me. Judging by the noise coming from the kitchen, I could only assume everyone else was already awake, and with their heightened hearing, I could only guess that they had indeed. I hesitated about going out, not wanting to face any of them. Forest stepped out behind me and looked down the hall towards the noise. He wrapped his arm around my waist in a reassuring gesture and led me to the bathroom.

Once we were showered and dressed for the day, we joined the others, partaking in the simple breakfast they had prepared with the food they had brought. I was relieved no one commented about Forest's and my activities this morning. The conversations that did happen had an overall uneasiness to them as the warriors prepared for the day. They had trained for this sort of thing, however. When faced with an unknown adversary, one that had already claimed the life of one of their fellow warriors, there was still some uncertainty. Forest, through, walked to the door with his head held high as if nothing fazed him.

"Time to train," he directed as he stepped out the door.

The others followed quietly. I stood on the porch and watched as they disappeared down the trail, their forms becoming only shadows amongst the trees. I returned to the room and quickly cleaned up the last few plates left out before grabbing my jacket and heading to my family's home. The snow crunched beneath my feet as I walked through the garden.

"It's Brave of you to go in there right now," a voice behind me said before I reached the small wooden porch.

I turned around to find Heather standing on the other side of the gate. We had spent very little time together since my return, and I felt she had been avoiding me.

"Do you think Violet is still angry?" I asked her.

"You know my mother. She's a stubborn old crow."

She was right; Violet was not one to let things go, but that would be a problem for another time. We stood there awkwardly for a moment before she continued.

"I'm on your side on this. My mother is over her head with... whatever this thing is. Thank you for doing what needs to be done. You're one of the only ones brave enough to stand up to her."

I was shocked by her testament.

"You're welcome," was the only response I could articulate.

She smiled weakly at me. I turned back around, and the two of us walked into the house together. Gran was finishing making breakfast when we came in.

"Hello, darlings," she called, "come have a seat."

We all took our seats at the table. I looked up as Violet walked in. She cast me an angry stare as she made her way over to her chair. Gran placed the dishes at the center of the table and took her place at the far end.

"Dig in," she said with a smile.

The towering food dishes were passed around, yet I took only a few pieces of fruit.

"Are you not hungry?" Gran asked me.

"I already ate."

"I didn't know you had food up there. I was planning on making those warriors of yours some breakfast once we were done."

"Thank you, but they are already out for the day."

"So early," she said, surprised, as she passed the bowl of oatmeal to Meadow.

"They are training before going out tonight," I told her.

"So they're going after the beast tonight?" Meadow asked from across the table.

"Yeah. They are heading out at dusk," I answered, trying to hide my sadness and fear.

"Wouldn't night be more difficult for them?" She asked further.

"Wolves have good night vision. It doesn't impede them. Plus, they wanted time to train on tactics to fight this thing."

"Where are they training? I feel like I should see if they need anything," Meadow said excitedly.

"You will stay away from those shifters," Violet scorned her.

"I was just trying to be a good host, Grandma," she said defensively.

"We all know what you wanted to do," Violet said with distaste. This is another reason why we should not have allowed them onto our land. They will lure our young girls into their promiscuous ways."

"That's enough, Violet," Gran said sternly at her.

Silence overtook the table as the two sisters stared off. I had become tired of the tensions in my family home.

"Can we call a meeting today? They asked if we can strengthen the ward while they fight the creature. They want to ensure that the coven is protected if it slips past them."

"If they need our help, then they obviously can't even perform the job that you ensured us that they would complete," Violet ridiculed.

I slammed my hands down on the table and stood up.

"This is not their fight! They do not have to be here. They are only here because I have asked them. I do not want to see my family, my coven, fall to some monster. The least you can do is show a sliver of respect, Some common decency."

I could feel the other's eyes on me, but I paid them no attention as I stormed away. Violet needed to reel herself in. I walked through the village center, where the others were starting to practice their spells. I took the path to the woods, never slowing in my rage-filled stride. I passed the newest ward the elders had placed that circled the settlement, feeling the slight tingle as I crossed. When the all too familiar meadow finally broke into my sight, I stopped and leaned on a tree. The warriors were training in the snow-covered field. It was near the last ward, dividing us from the creature that stalked our land.

I watched as they practiced their maneuvers against a giant stickman they had assembled with the intent of avoiding a long reach. The placement of sticks and branches was eerily similar to the actual monster, down to the claws and antlers. Forest stood at the center, directing them as they came after it one at a time. He instructed them to go for the legs first to incapacitate it, followed by the back.

I watched for hours before I heard someone approaching from behind. I turned to look and saw Meadow walking towards me.

"I don't think Violet will approve of you being here," I smirked at her.

"Yeah, yeah. My grandma has a stick stuck somewhere, if you know what I mean," she said, rolling her eyes.

"What's with her anyway?" I asked more seriously.

"I don't know. I don't think anyone knows," she sighed.

We stood there and watched the wall of muscular men mixed with wolves running around the field before us.

"I could watch this all day," she joked.

"I bet you could."

"Yeah," she laughed, "but I actually came here to talk to you. I just got...distracted."

I smiled at her, "What do you want to talk about?"

"I wanted to check on you," she smiled softly. "You seemed pretty heated at the house."

I sighed deeply, "I just don't understand why she dislikes the shifters so much. They are here to help, not hurt us."

"My grandma has always been resistant to change, you know that," she tried to explain.

"I know, but this is something bigger than us, and it doesn't hurt to accept help. They are part of me, the same as the coven. Does she not trust me?"

"She does. I think she feels powerless and is taking it out on you."

Well, it sucks," I told her.

"It does," she agreed as we returned to watching the warriors.

After a few minutes, she squeezed my hand and perked up, " I forgot to tell you. Your Gran requested a coven meeting. Everyone will be there in about an hour."

I turned to look at her. I had been so upset with Violet's crude remarks that I avoided the coven altogether. I was eternally grateful that my Gran stepped in for me and requested the meeting.

"I guess we should head back then!"

"Maybe in a few minutes. This is so much better than the movies we've seen."

I laughed and pushed my shoulder into hers. I missed my time with Meadow. She could always make me smile, no matter the situation.

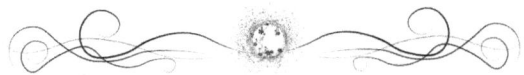

24

Forest

I followed Juniper into the coven's meeting hall. Only August and I would join her for their meeting. She came to ask for their help strengthening the ward. We stood at the back of the room as a steady stream of women made their way through the double doors and took their seats. I looked over the elders, trying to read their views of us being here. As far as I could tell, Violet was the only one who opposed our presence.

Violet stood and spoke to the room, "Sisters, we are gathered here today to hear a request from Juniper."

Juniper walked up the center aisle and stood before the elders. I was proud of how confident she held herself. Even through the bond, I felt no hesitation or nervousness.

"I have come to ask for the coven's help tonight while the West Moon Pack goes after the creature. We ask that the coven help strengthen the ward as a safety precaution in case it is able to pass them."

"The only way for us to do that would be to stand at the ward," Elder Pearl noted.

"Yes. We would like anyone in the coven who is able to cover the entire outer perimeter."

"That could provoke the beast further," Elder Briar said.

"We would remain hidden until the fighting has already begun. The creature will be distracted by the pack."

"It has already broken two barriers. What is to say that it will not cross another? Perhaps it is a good plan," Pearl suggested.

"It is too great of a risk," Violet added authoritatively. "We cannot allow you to endanger our coven further."

"I am not endangering anyone," Juniper argued back. "I am trying to do everything I can to protect them."

The elders gathered behind their table and whispered in conversation before returning to their seats.

"We disapprove of your plan. You have already convinced us that the pack will protect us. If they are unable, then they should not be here," Violet said smugly.

"Should we not work together?" Juniper added. "The more we can do, the more we work together, the stronger we will be."

"Our answer is no. Do not push our decision," Violet stared her down with a threat.

I could feel Juniper's anger and disappointment through the bond. She turned and walked back.

Violet addressed the coven, "With tonight's activities, all of you should stay within your homes. Be prepared for anything."

With that the meeting ended. Juniper was the first out the door. August and I followed her back to her mother's home to meet with the others. Dusk was nearly upon us.

I LED my group in the same direction we had gone several nights ago, circling outside the coven's land. However, we turned East earlier to account for the lost ward. We laid in wait once more for our enemy's arrival. Juniper had said it had been a quiet day and only felt it once around lunchtime to the North, returning to its normally consistent location. The cloud-covered night sky and the fresh blanket of snow muffled most noises, making our scenery eerily quiet. A chill of warning ran down my spine, putting my guard up.

No signs on our end, August checked in from his position in the trees near the meadow.

Neither on ours.

The hours slowly ticked by, and I began to fear it would not show up tonight following the quiet day. Perhaps it had come across something else? Or an even more terrifying thought, it could be trying to give us a sense of security. We were unsure of how intelligent this creature was. For the most part, it had returned to the same spot each time. Its appearance was more animal than man, but we could not allow ourselves to underestimate it again.

It's broken the ward! Juniper yelled through the link.

How? We have not seen or heard it yet.

It came from the East.

Dammit!

Everyone to the East, it's through the ward.

We took off running as fast as our legs would carry us. I flew ahead of my group, not wasting a moment getting to Juniper.

Juniper

I stood at the edge of the inner ward with Cole and the others. I could not bring myself to wait inside with the rest of the coven while Forest was out there. I paced back and forth with nervousness.

"Why don't you go in?" Cole suggested.

"Could you wait inside?" I asked him, annoyed.

He lowered his head, "No, Luna."

"I will stay here as long as..."

I nearly lost my footing when a massive pressure pushed me from my right.

"Luna?" Cole asked at my sudden stop in conversation.

It's broken the ward! I linked Forest.

How? We have not seen or heard it yet.

It came from the East.

"The beast has broken through on the East. We must defend the coven," I yelled at the men around me.

"Yes, Luna," they all yelled before the sound of ripping clothing echoed.

Each of them shifted into their wolves, and they began heading to the East. I followed suit, shifted, and chased after them. I took the lead, ensuring they went in the right direction. I knew these woods better than any of them. I saw several of my coven sisters running out of their houses towards the main hall as we passed them—a look of fear plastered upon their faces. We stopped just short of the ward in wait. It was only minutes before a black shadow came rushing through the trees. It was coming fast and heading straight for us.

We must stop him before he breaks the last ward, I told my pack members.

There were only five of us, one fewer than when Forest had fought it the other night. The odds were against us, but we had to try. I jumped past the ward and growled at the grotesque beast that emerged from the trees. Cole pushed in front of me, creating a barrier between us. The others followed. I watched as it barreled towards us in almost slow motion. Each step slammed into the ground and sent the snow flying around. The others jumped forward to circle it. It stopped as its mangled head turned slightly as it noticed the wolves behind it. When the first warrior jumped forward, going for the back of its legs, it moved at an impossible speed, swinging its arm back and knocking him away.

The others took turns diving in for it's legs, each being tossed to the side or slashed. I watched as, one by one, they crumbled under their injuries. I shifted back and stood tall, calling the same fireball as before. As the swirl of flame formed in my hand, the creature's head twisted toward me and began to race in my direction. It was right in front of me before I could even swing my arm. The fireball flew to the side, hitting one of the nearby trees. A cloud of snow showered down from its impact. I watched as it pulled its massive arm back, intending to bring it down on me. I attempted to dive backward but felt a sharp pain as its claws sliced through the skin on my arm and waist before I fell to the ground.

The three remaining wolves jumped onto its back, pulling it away from me. As I sat up, I felt a cold wind hit my back, and I turned around to see Violet standing on the other side of the ward, pushing her hands in our direction. I had never been so grateful to see her before. While the wind was mighty, it did little to the creature. The distance was too great, and the wind was dying off before it could make an impact. The creature's claws tore through Cole's shoulder, and he was tossed to the side before it noticed Violet squared off with it.

It shook its back and swung its powerful antlers around,

tossing the remaining warriors clear of it before running straight at her. I pulled myself up in an attempt to help, but my injury slowed me, and I watched in horror as it ran straight through the ward, only slowing for a moment at its resistance. I wanted to look away as there would be nothing preventing it from killing her right there, but as it charged forward, its head down and antlers at the ready, a flash of color came from Violet's side.

Heather...

She dove in front of the creature right as it reached Violet, taking the full force of its penetrating blow. When it stood up, Heather was impaled on its antlers, her blood dripping down onto its face. Violet screamed and threw her hands forward again, knocking the beast down with her mighty wind. Heather's crumpled body rolled off into the snow, leaving a bloody trail in its wake.

Drake, the last wolf standing, pounced on it once more. I pulled myself up to standing and called forth the flames, twirling them in my hands. As it clawed away at Drake, who had latched onto its back, I sent the fireball hurtling in the monster's direction, hitting it on the side of its head. The sharp, acidic smell of burnt fur quickly reached my nose on the breeze. As the creature stumbled backward, Drake detached himself and limped behind it, his hackles raised.

The creature righted itself, and its empty eyes stared straight at me. I knew I was its next target and prepared myself for battle. My hands were warm with energy as I called my powers to them. Drake attacked its back again, but the creature moved too fast, twisting around. Drake's injured legs slowed his response to the counter-attack, and claws struck with precision as they sliced through his throat, killing him instantly.

Rage boiled inside of me as I watched and felt my pack

member's life be stolen away. I threw another flaming orb at it, catching its arm, but failed at slowing its movements. It turned back towards me and charged at full speed. It took a flying leap right at me. I was sure it would kill me with its strike, but a second before impact, Forest's black wolf flew through the air, knocking them both to the side. They tumbled across the crimson ground, snow flying into the air. Forest quickly jumped up and attacked the creature before it could right itself. His claws tore away at its rotten flesh, and his head shook from side to side with a jaw full of the monster's decrepit hide. The creature howled its whistling call into the air before reaching over its shoulder and grabbing Forest's head.

I threw another ball of fire as quickly as I could create one, striking it in its chest. It barely reacted to the hit, and I knew we were in trouble. Panic filled me as I watched it pull Forest over in front of it, its claws tearing at the side of his face. I ran at it, shifting as I went and latched onto its arm. It dropped Forest to the ground and grabbed ahold of my abdomen, claws slicing into me. The yelp my wolf made forced my grip to release. Forest lunged once more, biting into the arm that held me, causing it to release me, and I fell with a hard thud to the ground. I could barely stand from the pain that was overtaking my body.

I could hear the thunder of paws coming from my side as the rest of the warriors broke through the trees, attacking the creature from all sides. Even with their relentless onslaught, the monster fought as if it instantly healed from the wounds inflicted upon it. The warriors, my pack, were slowly being taken out of the fight by this monster as I watched on in horror. Violet had snuck up to me and was trying to pull me away. I saw behind her the other elders putting a new ward up. They were placing themselves across the barrier to strengthen it.

"We must go. The coven cannot help us. They are using their power to strengthen the ward," Violet told me as I pulled against her.

I could not leave my pack. I shifted back, using her arm to help pull myself up.

"I'll be fine. I cannot leave the others. Help them," I told her.

She looked like she would fight my reply, but instead, she released my arms and ran behind the newly formed ward, joining the others. I pulled myself up on a nearby tree, feeling the depth of my injuries. I willed myself to help in the fight, no matter the cost. My knees nearly buckled beneath me as I watched Forest's wolf fly into a tree.

Fire, an ethereal voice whispered in my ear.

It was not like the mind-link but as if the voice had been carried in on the wind. I looked around, unable to find a source.

You must burn the heart, it said further.

I took an unsteady step forward.

"Clear the beast," I called out.

I watched as several wolves took a hesitant step back.

What are you doing? Forest asked me worriedly.

Trust me.

You heard your Luna. Clear the beast! He linked to our warriors.

They moved further back, watching the scene in front of them. The monster righted itself once more. It looked at the retreating wolves, but its eyes stopped at me. I slowly stepped forward, feeling the blood pouring down my side.

I took a long, deep breath and closed my eyes, my palms facing forward as I called my power from inside of me. I could hear the creature moving towards me, but I would not lose my concentration. I thought of its body, starting with its hoofed feet and moving up through its wolf-like legs.

You have to do something, Forest linked me.

I could feel his panic build, but I stood my ground. My thoughts continued up its protruding ribs, long arms with yellowed claws, hunched-over shoulders, and elk-like head. I focused on its heart, feeling only ice. I could hear its footsteps nearly in front of me. Another sound of footsteps began to race from my side.

Stop it! Forest screamed through the link.

As I heard them all begin to descend on the creature, I knew his orders were for the warriors.

"*Feumaidh cridhe deigh losgadh le teine. Thoir dhomh an tiodhlac seo, Selene gus stad a chuir air an uilebheist seo,*" I spoke with complete certainty.

I felt a cloud of snow fly into the front of my body. I opened my eyes to see the monster crumpled at my feet. Everyone stopped. Everything was silent. The only sound that came was a last whistling howl from the creature, but even then, as it opened its mouth, flames flew out from within it. In only a few seconds, the fire cut through its skin, igniting the entire form of the monster. The smell of rotting flesh being cooked filled the forest, making me wrinkle my nose in disgust. We all stood still as we watched the ash from the last lick of flame drift into the sky, becoming lost in the wind.

Forest shifted and walked up to me, pulling me tightly to him. I winced in pain from my still unhealed injuries.

"You did it," he whispered in my ear.

"I did," I said. I felt immensely proud of myself but also surprised by what I had accomplished. Where was this power coming from, and why was Selene talking to me? Was she answering my prayers for help? Or was there something more?

All of my questions would have to wait to be answered as now I needed to focus on those in front of me. Those who had fought and those we had lost. Pain tore at my heart as I looked over at Heather's lifeless body and to that of Drake's. Without their sacrifices, where would we have been? Violet was draped over Heather, her cries of grief sweeping through the trees.

Forest's strong arms swept under my legs and lifted me from the ground.

"Collect the fallen and bring them to the main hall," Forest called to his men.

As he began walking back to the settlement, I stopped him and said, "Wait. I need to help Violet."

He slowly let me back down but kept a firm hand at my waist to steady me as we approached her. August stood behind her with two other warriors.

"Violet, let them take her home," I spoke softly to her.

"Why would she do this? Why would she sacrifice herself for me?" she cried into Heather.

I gently rested my hand on her shoulder, "You're her mother. She couldn't bear losing you."

"I would rather her lose me than I lose her. She has children to care for. She had so much life ahead of her."

I kept my hand on her until her sobs softened, and she sat up, finally allowing the warriors to carry Heather's body back to the settlement. She looked at me with a heavy heart before following behind them. Forest lifted me again and took me back to where the rest of the coven had already come together to help heal those who had fought for them.

25

Juniper

We walked down to the center of the village towards the raging bonfire. I was dressed in my robe with a black dress flowing underneath. The warriors trailed behind us, an aura of sadness within all of them. When we arrived, my coven sisters parted, allowing us into their circle.

"Thank you for coming," Violet spoke to them with sorrow heavy in her voice.

Forest nodded to her. He squeezed my hand before he and the warriors circled outside the coven. I walked over to Meadow and took her hand in mine. I could see the tears spilling from her heavy green eyes.

"We come together to pass our sister, our mother, our daughter back to Selene. It is within her home that Heather Nary will find peace once more."

Several women came in from the side, carrying a wooden platform. Heather's wool-wrapped body sat on top of it, covered with evergreen branches, winterberries, and snowdrops. Candles were perched along the edges. They entered the circle and placed the platform down on four posts around the fire. Within several minutes, the flames began to engulf her form.

"Luaith gu luaithre, duslach gu duslach. Bheir Selene do nighean dhachaigh," Violet chanted, raising her arms to the sky.

We each repeated her, our arms lifting to the heavens. A harmonious chorus began to fill our settlement as we each began to sing.

"*Selene ar màthair, tha sinn air do shon. Do chlann an seo agus an-dràsta. Bheir sinn sinn fhìn dhut gu bràth is barrachd, a-nis thoir do leanabh dhachaigh.*"

"*Selene, our mother, we are for you—your children here and now. We give you ourselves forever and more. Now take your child home.*"

Our song continued until Heather was no more. She had been returned to Selene to live eternally by her side. I turned to Meadow and pulled her into me. She sobbed heavily into my shoulder. I held her tightly even as the rest of the coven returned to their homes. All that was left was the Nary clan. I turned to Forest, giving him a nod towards the houses. He took my lead and led the warriors away.

"Family..." Violet began, "We are family. I am sorry for allowing our disagreements to come between us."

She looked at me, "I am sorry I did not trust our own."

I stepped to her and held her hands within mine.

"I am sorry for the loss of your only daughter. Heather was a woman to be proud of."

"She was," she agreed solemnly.

A unified sadness filled the air as we each looked at one another.

"We have had much hardship within our house. Two

lives were taken early," Violet said as she looked at my Gran. "Without Juniper, chances are that all of us could have been taken. We thank you for never turning away from us, even when we pushed."

"I never will," I told her.

"Let us go find warmth within our home," my Gran told us.

We followed each other across the small wooden bridge and up the trail. Once we had settled into the living room, Violet stood near the fireplace.

"With your mother gone, Meadow and Willow will move into the Nary home. Wren, since you are with child, you can take ownership of your mother's house."

"I already have a house being built. I don't need it," Wren said.

"Then it shall sit empty until one of your sisters starts a family of their own."

"No," Meadow objected. "My mother would not want her home to become dark."

"It is our custom. Only our sisters with children may have a place of their own."

"Then I will take it," said Wren." When the time comes, the home being built can go to one of my sisters.

"If that is what you wish," Violet told her. "I know this is not easy, my children, but it is our way. Juniper, since you no longer reside in your room, perhaps you would be willing to pass it to one of your cousins?"

"Of course I will. I have been staying at my mother's house anyway."

"Meadow, perhaps you would like it?" Violet asked her.

Meadow looked at me for approval. I smiled compassionately at her. Though I had been young, I still remember being brought into the family home. My room brought me comfort, and while Meadow is an adult, hopefully, she can find the same retreat I had within it.

"Yes, I will take Juniper's room."

"Willow, you may take the spare room. We will move your belongings in the morning."

I wished Violet had given them more time before making such drastic changes in their lives, but as she said, it was our way. The coven always believed that it was better to feel all of your grief at once rather than drag it out. If she had given them more time, it would only have caused their pain to resurface again and again.

I said my farewells and walked up to my mother's house. It was a welcomed feeling to find it lit and full of life. I hung my coat and walked over to Forest, resting my head against his chest.

"We are sorry for your loss, Luna," August said quietly.

I lifted my head to look at him and then across the crowded room.

"We have all lost. While Heather was mine to lose, we all lost Dylan, Talon, and Drake. Three of our warriors lost to this monster. I feel each and everyone, and I thank each of you for risking your lives for my family."

"You are our Luna," Cole stepped forward. "Your family is our own."

I smiled solemnly at him, "And your family is mine."

"Come, we all must rest so we can return home tomorrow," Forest interjected.

He took my hand and led me down the hallway into my mother's old room. After untying my cloak and hanging it on a hook on the back of the door, he lifted my heavy black dress over my head. I knew that this was done out of care. He finished undressing me before sliding my soft cotton pajamas on and carried me to the bed. Now that it was just us, hidden away on our own, I let myself cry. He held me tightly through the night, even after I had drifted off to sleep.

"Don't take too long before you come back again," my Gran told me as she kissed me on the cheek.

"I won't," I smiled back at her.

We hugged tightly before she stepped back. Meadow stood to her side. We hugged next.

"Call me anytime. Even though I'm not at the coven, I'm still here for you," I told her.

"I know, and I will," she said.

It seemed like the fire that normally burned within her had been nearly snuffed out by the loss of her mother. She would recover in time, but it would be a difficult road for her to get there. It would be hard for the whole coven to recover after the beast. But hopefully, day by day, life will return to normal for them, as it will for me.

I climbed into the front passenger side of Forest's car. August and Cole were in the back. We needed room in the back of one of the SUVs to bring our warriors home for their own funerals. I did not look forward to talking to Drake's mate. They had three small children at home. Forest had offered to speak to her on his own, but since he had died fighting for my family, it only felt fitting that it should be me who delivered the news on how it happened. She would have already felt the bond break, knowing that she lost her mate. I couldn't even imagine the heartbreak she was feeling.

The drive was peaceful. I spent most of the time watching the scenery pass by us. After we passed through

Vancouver and turned into the mountains, I finally felt some relief. Home... we were home. While the coven was where I grew up and was packed full of nostalgia and comfort, the West Moon Pack had become my home. The others held back to give us time to talk to Jade, Drake's mate. We drove down the main street, which on its own drew attention. While some cars were parked throughout the town, they were more for show than practicality since we rarely left.

We pulled up in front of a quaint craftsman-style home with bright cedar shingles on the upper half.

"Juniper," Forest started before we climbed out of the car. "You need to remember what the mate bond does. Most wolves cannot survive without their mate. You need to be prepared."

I swallowed the lump that had formed in my throat.

"Do they ever survive?"

"Rarely..."

I hesitantly stepped out of the car, my heart breaking for Drake's family. As we walked up the walkway, the front door opened, and Rosemary, Jade's mother, stepped out with a solemn look on her face.

"How is she?" Forest asked as we approached.

"Not well. Beta Oakley brought me over after the neighbors called about screams coming from her house."

She stepped back, holding the door open for us.

"Please help her, Alpha. She has not even looked at her children since she felt the bond break."

"We will do everything we can," he said to her as we stepped inside.

I looked around the room, noting the baby bouncer and toys tucked against the walls. The vice around my heart tightened.

"Where are the children?" I asked her.

"My other daughter, Sage, has them. It does them no good to see her like this."

I nodded my head at her.

"May I check on her?" I asked the older woman.

"Yes, Luna. She is upstairs, first door on the left."

"Thank you."

I slowly walked up to the darkened staircase, finding her door closed. I stood outside it for a moment, listening, before knocking lightly. When there was no answer, I slowly turned the knob and peeked inside. The bed was unmade but empty. I looked across the dark room and spotted her sitting in the corner, her kneels pulled tightly to her chest.

"Jade?" I called to her.

She did not move. I stepped inside and closed the door behind me.

"Jade," I called again, but there was still no response.

I edged closer to her, kneeling in front of her. There was no reaction.

"I cannot imagine what you are feeling right now. I have not experienced your pain, only that of losing my mother. Even then, I was a small child. Is there anything I can do for you?"

She still did not respond. Unsure what to do, I sat down all the way, crossing my legs over each other. If she could not respond or did not want to talk, perhaps I could just be here for her.

"I am here for you, Jade," I whispered softly.

I tried to reach towards her, but just as I was about to touch her, she recoiled and bared her teeth at me. I realized now that her wolf was in control. I pulled my hand back quickly.

"I understand you do not wish to be touched. I will respect that."

She buried her face back into her knees, tightening her arms around them. We sat silently for a while. Every so often, I spoke to her, but I received no response.

I need to talk to the other families. The caravan has returned, Forest linked me.

Go, I am going to stay here for a while, I told him.

I would prefer you to come with me. Those who have lost their mate can be volatile, he urged,

I'll be fine, I assured him.

I will send Oakley to wait outside.

If that makes you feel better, I sighed through the bond.

It does... He adamantly responded.

I fought back the smile but remembered where I was and kept it hidden.

"Jade, would you like some water? Or food?"

Her silence continued.

The shortened days of winter brought an early nightfall. Jade and I remained unmoved. I watched as her back moved slightly with each breath, but other than when she lashed out at me, she sat perfectly still. It pained me to see her in so much grief, something that was caused by her mate protecting my coven. I needed to do something, but what could I do?

My Gran had once told me that there were ways to lessen one's grief, but we did not follow it as my coven believed that it was a pain that must be felt. We never experienced loss such as this, however. Our pain could be harsh, such as Meadow losing her mother. Having experienced the mate bond, I knew it was so much more than any connection a human or even a witch would feel. We say that when we find our mate, we suddenly feel complete. They are the other half of our souls. What happens when someone loses that part? Are we left with half a soul? Half a

Heart? Perhaps I could lessen her pain. I had no incantation for it, but like many I had cast over the last half a year, maybe it would just come to me. Spells were always most potent if we touched those we were casting on. After her previous reaction, I knew I would only get one chance at this.

"Jade, I can try to ease your pain. Would you like me to do that?" I asked her.

With her silence, I flexed my fists a few times, mentally preparing myself. I reached forward, grabbing ahold of her hand. She lashed out, screeching and trying to claw at me, but I wrapped my arms around her. I closed my eyes and focused as best I could.

"*Cha tèid cràdh aon uair air chall air a dhìochuimhneachadh, slànaich an t-anam seo agus thoir beatha a-staigh,*" I spoke quickly, releasing her just as the door flew open.

Oakley came rushing into the room, followed by Rosemary. They looked us over, finding Jade weeping in her hands.

"Jade," her mother called as she rushed over to her. She stayed back a step, showing her wisdom about the situation.

"I can't believe he is gone," she cried forcefully.

"Oh, Jade," Rosemary said as she dropped to her knees and pulled her daughter into her arms.

Oakley and I took this as our time to leave. We quietly slipped out, and he walked me back to the packhouse.

"What happened in there? I can't believe she is talking," he asked me with disbelief.

"What do you mean?"

"Usually, a wolf never recovers from the loss of their mate. They slowly drift farther and farther away until nothing is left of them. They either starve themselves or take their own lives, unable to continue on."

I bit my lip and peeked over at him, "Well...I may have helped her."

He stopped walking and looked at me, "What do you mean?"

"I gave her a healing spell," I looked at him worried.

I had never liked casting spells on someone without their permission. I never wanted to cross a boundary.

"You can do that?" He asked, stunned.

I shrugged, "I guess so..."

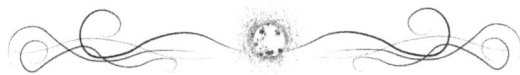

26

Forest

I lay in bed beside Juniper, watching as she got comfortable. I had thought I lost her back in the woods when the creature made its final charge. Several times, really. First, when I felt her pain before I could get to her, and second, when she called us off, and it went after her. I don't know what I would have done if I had lost her.

"You never did tell me how you defeated the creature..."

"I don't know, there was a voice. The same one as when I found you the first time you encountered the creature. It told me what to do."

"Whom's voice do you think it was?"

"I don't know. I've thought that maybe Selene is leading me. She has helped me before."

"Does her voice sound the same?"

"In a way, it has the same ethereal quality, but it was carried on the wind or something."

"Why do you think she is helping you?"

"Honestly, Forest," she looked intently at me, "I don't know. So much has happened, so much I can't explain. Why did she pull me to her after Sienna stabbed me? Why did she help me fight the monster? I wish I had an answer, but I don't."

"We will figure it out," I whispered, pulling her to me. I inhaled her lavender and honey scent, feeling her instant calming effect on me.

AUGUST KNOCKED on my open office door.

"Come in," I told him as I ran my hand down my face.

My eyes ached from reading each of the warriors' reports from our trip down to the coven. It had been two weeks since our return. A few days after we got back, we held funerals for our three fallen warriors. Oakley had informed me how Juniper was able to help Jade get past the initial break in her bond. While she had not fully gotten over the loss of her mate, she was able to care for her children again.

August sat across from me, "I think I may have found what the creature was."

He set a book on my desk, facing me, and pushed it over. I looked down at an artistic drawing of a creature that resembled the same thing we had faced—the same dark, sunken eyes, long, tangled antlers, and hoofed feet. I read the inscription below.

> The Wendigo - a cannibalistic creature that
> yields superior strength, speed, and a
> keen sense used to devour its victims.
> They inhabit cold environments in the

Canadian and North American
woodlands.

"A Wendigo? Do you think it really was one of these?"

"It looks and sounds just like it. It even says that the only way to kill it is to burn its ice-encased heart. If not for the Luna, we would never have defeated it."

Whatever the voice Juniper had heard had saved us once more.

"I had only known these to be a fable."

"Me too. I suppose if we shifters are real, there is no knowing what creatures really exist."

He had a point. We, too, are considered a story of lore, yet here we were.

"Are there any records of our pack having run into one before?"

"Not that I have found. This appears to be our first encounter with one."

"We need to leave a detailed record of it. If our pack ever faces one again, they will know what to do," I told him.

"Already on it, Alpha."

After August left, I picked up my office phone. The legends of the Wendigo originated with the native tribes. One of the northern packs we had a treaty with was of native origin. If I wanted more information beyond the single page in the book that August found, they would be an excellent place to start. The phone rang a few times before Beta Katjuk answered.

"Atelihai," he spoke through the phone.

"Hello, This is Alpha Forest from West Moon."

"Alpha Forest, what can I do for you today?"

"I have a question that I think you all may be able to help me with."

"Would you like to speak to Alpha Amaqjuaq?"

"It's possible you can help me so as not to bother the alpha. I was wondering if you know anything about Wendigos."

The line was silent for a moment.

"The kewok..." he finally responded.

"Is that a wendigo?" I asked.

"Yes, They are men and women whose souls are corrupted," he explained in his heavy accent.

"You mean that they are not their own creature?"

"No, they are lost souls taken by greed or unable to survive the winter. They target those disconnected from their communities, thirsting for their blood."

My memory of the creature biting into Dylan filled my thoughts.

"Why do you ask of the kewok?" Beta Katjuk asked seriously.

"We believe we had a run-in with one."

"If it knows of your location, you must be careful. Once it has a victim in sight, it is relentless until it finally succeeds," he warned.

"That won't be a problem. We killed it."

"They are nearly impossible to defeat! Only destroying its heart can kill it."

"We burnt its heart, the whole creature. It is gone," I assured him.

"I bow to your victory. It is not an easy task."

"It was not. You said that it goes after people who are disconnected. The one we found was attacking a village, a small one."

"One in the village has separated themselves from the rest. An outsider lost in the crowd. It would have sensed it amongst them. How large was it?"

"It was a behemoth. At least eight feet tall."

"Then it fed on many victims. They grow each time they consume, and their hunger is never satisfied."

"Do we need to be concerned that another one will come?"

"There are very few kewok. Once a soul begins to corrupt, it changes. Often, before they fully transform, they will begin attacking those around them, needing to feast. Once they have devoured their first victim, their body transforms into what I believe you saw. I would not expect you to find another, but there is always a chance."

"Thank you for your help, Beta Katjuk."

"You are welcome, Alpha. Be safe."

"You as well."

I hung up the phone and sat back in the chair. I wondered who within the coven the beast would have targeted. I decided to talk to Juniper about it. I left my office and found her in our apartment, curled up on the sofa with a book.

"What are you reading?" I asked her.

She smiled at me, "Just a little romance novel I found in the library."

I sat down next to her and wrapped my arm around her shoulders.

"We have found out what the creature was," I told her, getting straight to my point.

She sat up straight and looked at me, "What was it?"

"Something called a wendigo. I talked to another pack, who said they are corrupted souls that feast on weakened people."

"Why would it go after my coven then? They are not weak."

"Someone is. I was told that once the creature finds a victim, it will not stop until it devours them."

She held her hand over her mouth and took a sharp breath, "I, I don't know who that could have been. I mean, the whole coven is like a giant family."

"Has anyone been distant?"

"Well, Heather had been since she cast the spell on me. Do you think she was who it was after?"

"It could be. What about her daughters? Had she still been close with them?"

"As far as I know. Meadow never told me much about her mom since everything happened. I hope it wasn't Heather. She only did what she thought was right back then, even if what she did was wrong. Do you think that I did this?"

I stopped her, "No. This is not your fault. Even if it was Heather, she made her own choices."

"Choices that I forced upon her."

"This is not your doing, Juniper," I said, pulling her into me. "Maybe you should call your Gran and ask her. Perhaps she would have a better insight into who had become the outsider of the coven."

"Yeah...I will."

Juniper

AFTER FOREST LEFT, I pulled my cell phone from the desk and called my Gran.

"Hi, Gran," I said as I heard her pick up the phone.

"Oh, hello, darling. How are you?"

"I'm okay," I mumbled.

"What's wrong, my child?" she asked concerned.

"Gran, was Heather withdrawn from the coven over the last few months?"

"Not really. She was careful with what she was doing, never wanting to overstep, but she was right there with all of us. Why do you ask?"

"We think we found out what the creature that attacked the coven was. Apparently, it was after one of the coven sisters who was disconnected from the community. At least that is how Forest put it."

"Hmm, I would not say Heather was disconnected. In fact, she seemed to be finally finding her step again."

"Is there someone else you can think of who has been withdrawn?"

Gran was quiet for a while. I knew she was thinking it over.

"The only person who has not seemed, no, that can't be..."

"Who Gran?" I pushed her.

I could hear the breath she took before answering, "Well...Violet," she whispered.

"How could it be Violet? She seems like she is everywhere."

"Yes, but she has been doing so many things on her own. She might be everywhere, but she has been trying to lead independently from the rest of us. She is never in sync with the overall beliefs and thoughts of the community. You saw it yourself when you were here."

Violet opposed most of my ideas, but I assumed this was due to the situation and her determination to protect the coven in the way she saw fit.

"Is there a way to tell?" I asked her.

"Let me think...perhaps we can pull the coven's power. If her connection is weakened, then she does not have the full power of the coven behind her. It only happens if one separates themselves from us."

"Can you do it?"

"I can talk to the elders about our concerns."

"I think that is a good idea. I wouldn't think another creature would be out there, but we don't want to draw something like that to the coven again."

"I agree," she said with a hint of fear.

27

Juniper

Forest and I pulled into the coven's drive after making the long trek back down from our pack. After my Gran had spoken to the elders, it had been decided to pull power from the moon. They had said it would be best if I attended since I was part of the coven, and it would strengthen the spell if we were all together. It was hard to wait over a month before returning to the coven when I wanted to tackle this situation immediately. The next full moon after getting home to the pack had been the wolf moon, one most celebrated by shifters. We had a huge festival celebrating our connection as wolves to the moon goddess. Forest had refused to let me travel alone or even with a group of warriors like last time and instead insisted on coming with me.

Our arrival was just as celebrated as it had been each time we came. My coven sisters flooded out of their homes and down the glistening snow-packed trail to the end of the

rough gravel drive, where we parked our car. I climbed out
and saw my Gran hurrying towards me.

"Juniper," she said, kissing my cheeks. I'm so glad you're
here."

Forest grabbed our bag from the trunk, and we walked
up to my mother's house. I was surprised to see it freshened
up when we walked in. The curtains were open, shining the
bright day's light throughout the clean room. All of the little
clutter had been put away, and all of the surfaces were
freshly dusted. There was even a bowl of ripe fruit on the
counter.

"I thought I would make it a little homier for the two of
you," she chirped.

My mouth hung open. I turned to her and said, "Thank
you, Gran! You didn't need to do all of this."

She grinned at me, "It was no hassle. I'm happy to see
this place with a fresh light."

"Me too," I said, looking around once more.

After saying farewell to Gran, we headed down the hall
to put our bag away. We could only stay a single night,
which made my heart ache, but after spending so much
time with my family the month before last, even though it
had been under strenuous circumstances, I could not
complain. Forest had pressing work to attend to back at
West Moon, and I was grateful he made the trip with me to
my coven.

I looked over the brightly lit room with its wooden walls
and earthly paintings scattered around. I sighed deeply as a
slew of emotions coursed through me. It was a welcomed
feeling to be back in my mother's house, but I had always
assumed that I would one day live here with my own children. Instead, I lived over a hundred miles away with my
mate. I gazed over at Forest, who had placed our bag in the

wardrobe against the far wall. Warmth filled me as I looked over him. This may not have been the life I had expected, but it was one that I welcomed with open arms and a heart filled with gratitude. I walked over and wrapped my arms around his toned waist. He turned around within my grasp so that he could face me. He pushed a stray hair out of my face. The sparks from his touch ran through my body.

"You're utter perfection, Juniper," he spoke in a deep husky voice.

I bit my lip as a shiver ran up my body from his seductive tone. I could feel the warmth grow between my legs. Every time we stayed here in the past, besides the most recent, we stayed in the Nary house. I was too concerned that my Gran and the others would hear us, so we would sneak into the woods to spend our *alone* time together. I realized that being in my mother's old home, or what is essentially now my home, tucked away from the others, we no longer needed to sneak around like sex-crazed teenagers.

I stood up on my toes, kissing him deeply. His scent invaded my senses and only fueled me further. He hoisted me up, my legs wrapping around him. The entire world around us slipped away at that moment. It was only us, and nothing could get in our way. Forest took two giant steps to the bed and laid us upon it. His arm supported his weight so that he would not crush me. His hand roamed down my curves, his fingers teasing at the hem of my shirt. I gasped as his lips broke away from mine only to travel down the curve of my neck, his hot breath raking across my skin. His fingers quickly worked the button on my jeans and pulled them down my legs. I used my feet to kick them the rest of the way off as he returned to my soft folds that ached for him. His thumb ran between pushing down on my clit before giving it a slight pinch.

"F-forest," I called out as my back arched, and I thrust my hips into his hands, desperate for him to touch me deeper.

He growled as he heard his name, slipping two of his fingers within me. I gasped and rolled my head, savoring his touch. His hand moved in and out of me as his thumb continued to attack my clit. His free hand roamed upwards until he found my breast. He needed it within his grasp, and his mouth followed, taking in as much as possible. His tongue twirled around my nipple, and he bit down lightly, causing goosebumps to spread out across my skin. The unbearable pressure that built low in my stomach reached its tipping point as I finally released, coating his fingers in my juices. He pulled his fingers out and placed them in his mouth, cleaning them thoroughly. His eyes locked onto mine.

I needed him in me and was unwilling to wait a moment more. I grabbed hold of his pants, pulling him to me as I made quick work of them, pushing them down his powerful thighs. He could see my need and lust written all over my face as he smirked at me. He grabbed his shirt with one hand, pulling himself free of its confines. His large veined member stood proudly as he lowered back down above me. I could feel the tip butt up against my opening, and I widened my legs, welcoming him in. He kissed me deeply once more, thrusting his entire length into me. I gasped through his lips, greedily taking him wholly.

He pinned my hands above my head as I tightened my already quivering thighs around him. He slammed into me again and again, my body matching his movements, desperate for everything he would give. I was on the threshold of my release as he moved his head down to my mark and bit down deeply, implanting his canines into my skin. A euphoric blast of pleasure took hold of my body as I sucked air into my lungs, and my body came unraveled. I could feel my wetness drip down my thighs as my body began to settle.

He released my hands, and I pushed him over, climbing on top of him. I needed to take him as he had taken me. I slowly slid down his length, my walls clenching him as if they were embracing his presence. I rocked my hips, rolling my head back as I felt him grind across my cervix. He held my waist, nails digging into my skin as he watched me with lustful intent. He moved, synchronizing with my movements as I gained momentum. Harder and harder, I slammed my body down on his, the sound of skin slapping skin and our panted breaths echoed off of the walls. I could feel my claws lengthen as I held tightly to his shoulders, anchoring me down as my body began to spasm. I cried out loud with my release, feeling him spill within me at the same time.

I panted hot breaths on his chest as my body collapsed in on itself, his hands keeping me stable atop him. He moved me for a few more moments, making me let out a few small gasps. He kissed along the top of my shoulder as a shiver ran down the length of my spine.

"I will never tire of the way you feel, mate," he whispered into my ear.

I sat up slightly so that I could look him in my eyes, a smile across my lips, "Nor I you, my love."

We did not rush away from the bed but held still within each other's arms. I must have drifted off to sleep as the next thing I remembered, a light kiss brushed against my forehead, and I heard Forest whispering into my ear. I cracked open my eyes, taking note of the darkened room.

I jumped up, "What time is it?"

"Nearing ten."

"Dammit, why did you let me sleep?"

He grinned, "I tried to wake you, but you were out."

I hurried over to the wardrobe and pulled my robe out, throwing it over my shoulders. One good thing about our little escapade was that I was already undressed, though I would have preferred to shower and fix my hair. I could still feel the stickiness between my legs. I hurried down the hall into the bathroom and grabbed a towel, cleaning myself up the best that I could.

"I rather like my scent all over you," he teased me.

I glared at him through the mirror as I noticed my disheveled locks. I ran my fingers through my curls, attempting to tame them down.

"I would like my coven not to know what we have just done," I bit back at him.

"I'm sorry," he said with a mischievous smile, "Next time, I will make sure to wake you with plenty of time."

I scrunched my nose but took it as a win, even if he slightly mocked me. I straightened myself and grabbed his hand as I rushed back to the living room, slipping on my boots before heading out.

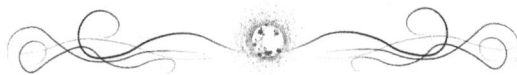

28

Juniper

We walked into the center of the settlement, the festivities already underway. The tables were nearly full, but I caught sight of Meadow and my Gran off to the side, waving us over. Forest took off to the food tables, and I watched as he prepared each of us a plate as I sat down next to Gran. Meadow kept her head down and pushed her food around her plate.

"How are you doing?" I asked her concerned.

Gran smiled sympathetically at her before looking back at me, "She's still working through the loss of Heather."

Meadow's eyes shot up, and she glared at Gran, "You all think it should be easy for us just to let her go. I know my mother made mistakes, but she was still my mother."

"Meadow," I started, but Gran gently squeezed my leg.

"Sweetheart, no one looked down on your mother. She was a strong witch and a wonderful mother. We all miss her. She sacrificed herself to save a coven sister, her own mother. No one would ever look down on her."

"Yet you all pushed us into moving into the main house. Not only have I lost my mother, but my home as well," she breathed out in anger.

"With each difficult task we face, our strength and power grow. I know it is hard, Meadow, but you will come to heal in time."

Meadow pushed her plate away and stormed away from the table. I was stunned. She had always been the optimistic one between the two of us. I could never remember a time when I had seen her so angry and sad. I began to stand to go after her, but my Gran held onto my hand.

"She needs time to process her loss, Juniper. Let her go."

"She needs a shoulder to cry on, Gran," I told her.

I followed Meadow out of the gathering and down the trail to the forest. My skin crawled from the recent memories of our encounter with the wendigo.

Keep Gran company; I need to check on Meadow, I linked Forest.

I was sure he had watched the encounter, but I needed to be sure he didn't follow.

I will, but don't go too far.

I smiled at his overprotective nature, *I won't.*

Once I broke through the tree line, I quickly found Meadow perched on a snow-covered fallen tree. I silently walked over and sat next to her. I could see the tears trailing down her cheeks and her fists clenched in her lap. She was in turmoil as she battled with her emotions. Still, I gave her time before pressing her.

"Is it true that someone brought the monster here?" she asked, her voice filled with anger and sorrow.

"From what we have found, the Wendigo feeds on outsiders within a community. It would have sensed someone that had separated themselves from the rest of us."

I wanted to be honest with her, knowing how the others would have approached the subject. They would tiptoe around her, trying not to bother her with facts. Having lost my mother, too, I knew that facts were what she needed to get through this.

"Who do you think it is?" she asked, keeping her sights on the ground, unwilling to look me in the eyes.

"My Gran thought perhaps Violet," I answered honestly.

Her head turned quickly, and she looked at me with shock. "My Grandmother? You think she brought that thing here?"

I looked at her sympathetically, "I don't know, but I do know that whoever brought it did not intend to. They might not even know that they have removed themselves from the coven, creating a risk to us all."

"It doesn't matter. Someone is responsible for my mother's death!"

"You're right, and that someone is the monster. I understand you're angry. Trust me, I don't blame you one bit for being angry. I'm angry, too. Your mom was like a surrogate mother to me. While we had a falling out, I still loved her."

She hunched over into her hands and began to sob. I wrapped my arm over her shoulders and pulled her to me, holding her through her grief.

After several minutes, her tears began to slow, "I just can't believe that she's gone."

"I know, me either, but you know what she would tell you if she were here?"

A slight chuckle slipped out between her sobs, "she would tell me to pick my butt up, brush myself off and look towards the moon."

I laughed alongside her, "Yeah, your mom was not one to

shy away from things. She took every challenge head-on,
very stubbornly, might I add."

"She did, didn't she."

I nodded, smiling at her, "And she would want you to do
the same."

"She never lost her mother," she said solemnly.

"No...she didn't."

We sat silently as the crisp breeze blew our hair into our
faces.

It looks like they are about to begin, Forest linked me.

We will be right there.

"They're starting," I told her.

She wiped the tears away from her eyes and hopped off
the tree. I jumped down next to her and wrapped my arm
over her shoulders again as we began the walk back. Purple
candles surrounded by jars of ice and flowing white flowers
graced the tables as we walked past them. The others had
already gathered around the fire. Violet stood proudly at the
front, waiting for the last of us. Meadow and I took our
places in the circle, our hands held together.

Violet stepped forward, "Tonight shall be slightly
different than our usual celebrations. We shall cast our
devotion to both Selene and our coven to the heavens for all
to see before we begin our ritual."

She raised her hands and began to chant, "A mhàthair, a
pheathraichean, tha sinn ceangailte riut. Faic leis an t-solus ar
dìlseachd do gach aon."

Each of us followed, repeating the words again and
again until I could feel my power pull from within me, like a
warm stream running through my veins. We swayed side to
side in unison as if a rope tethered our waists together. I
watched as slivers of light began to shine upwards into the
darkened night, one after the other. It was a kaleidoscope of

brilliance dancing overhead. Pearl and Briar stood side by side. I noticed them nod to each other before stepping away from the gathering and walking around the circle, inspecting each coven sister's light. Pearl smiled as she crossed me. I looked up to see a powerful blue light coming from me. I peeked over at Violet just as Briar came face to face with her. Her disappointed look told Violet everything we suspected. Her dim light shone weakly next to all the others.

Even though Gran had suggested it, I had thought there was no way it could have been her. She was the leader of the elders, yet she held the weakest bond to our sisterhood. Briar took her hand and led her away towards the main hall.

Pearl stepped forward and smiled at the coven, "It is a wonder to see our connection to not only Selene but to one another. Let us now devote ourselves to our mother."

The lights in the sky began to flicker out as the chant tapered off.

Pearl raised her hands again to the moon and chanted to the heavens, *"Le plaide blàths na gealaich sneachda seo, tha sinn a' cur fàilte oirbh nar cridheachan."*

She dropped her cloak, hands lifted to the sky as we followed her lead, repeating the incantation. We began to dance around the flickering flames, twirling and weaving around each other, celebrating Selene and our connection to her. However, my mind continued to wander back to Violet. What was to become of her? I looked over at Meadow, who had noticed as well. Though she danced, her heart was not in it. I looked back at Forest, who was sitting at the tables, his eyes locked onto my body as it swayed around the fire.

"Come on," I told her, grabbing her hand.

We needed to know what they were planning on doing.

Forest followed us as I led Meadow towards the main hall. I pushed the doors open, revealing the nearly empty room. Violet was sitting in a chair front and center facing the elder's table, where Briar sat. I felt warmth as my cloak was carefully draped over my shoulders. I looked back to see Forest wink at me. He helped Meadow with hers as well. I knew any other time it would have made her giddy, yet the circumstances in front of us would not allow it from her.

"Ladies, you should return to the celebration," Briar spoke with command.

"No," Meadow said sternly, surprising me. "I need to see her."

She walked up and around the chair so that she could face her grandmother. I saw her anger soften when she looked down on her face.

"Grandma..." she whispered.

"I'm so sorry, my child," Violet sobbed, "I did not realize that I had brought such evil upon us. I-it took my daughter, my baby."

Violet's shoulders bounced as she wept. Meadow dropped down in front of her, hugging her tightly. After a minute, she turned back to Briar.

"What will happen to her?"

"The elders will meet tonight to discuss the issue."

As if on cue, the doors behind us opened, and the other elders walked in, draped in their cloaks, their hoods hiding their faces. Their look was ominous as they passed Forest and me, leading up to the table where they each took a seat. They pulled their hoods down, revealing their unhappy gazes directed at Violet.

"We figured this should be settled right away as we saw Juniper and yourself come in," Pearl directed at Meadow.

Meadow nodded her head and stood up, taking a step back.

"Violet, you have endangered our coven with your greed for power and control. According to our laws, you are hereby stripped of your title as Nary Elder; the title is to be passed to the next in succession."

Gran. She would be the new Nary elder.

Pearl continued, "Tomorrow morning, we shall hold a meeting to put it to vote on whether you shall remain in our coven or be banished from our lands."

Violet's head dropped in defeat. My heart felt for her. She had just discovered that it was she who had brought forth the beast that killed her daughter, and now her standing in the coven was to be stripped away.

"Violet, you will be bound to your room until tomorrow's meeting. The rest of us shall return to the celebration."

The elders stood. Briar and Olive led Violet out the doors, her head hung low. Pearl walked up to us, sympathy heavy in her eyes as she looked over Meadow.

"You can't banish her," Meadow pleaded.

"It is not up to any one of us to decide. It must be made as a coven. I'm sorry, Meadow," Pearl answered.

Pearl and the remaining elders took their leave, taking Violet with them, and left us alone in the hall.

"Do you want to go back up to the house?" I asked Meadow, knowing that celebrating when she had just learned that she might lose her grandmother as well could be too much for her.

She sighed, "Yeah. I'm not in the mood to celebrate."

~

THE FOLLOWING MORNING, the coven gathered within the hall. I spotted my Gran seated at the elder's table and sent her a tight smile. Word had spread about Violet's connection to the coven and her part in bringing the wendigo to our lands. The room was flooded with whispers and gossip as Pearl stood from the elder's table, raising her hands to silence the room.

"As many of you have heard, Violet Nary was found to have a weakened bond to our coven. We had received word that the creature that had haunted our lands was, in fact, a Wendigo. A vile creature that feeds on those separated from their communities. I ask that Alpha Forest of the West Moon Pack step forward to inform us of his findings."

I looked over at Forest, who had already been notified that they intended for him to speak. He walked to the front and faced the elders, relaying his source and the information he had gathered. Gasps and crying could be heard as he detailed the carnage the wendigo could bestow. After answering all of their questions, he returned to my side, giving me a reassuring look. Everyone turned as the doors opened, and two coven sisters led Violet down the center row to stand before the elders.

Pearl stood again, "Violet Nary, do you wish to address the coven?"

She turned to face the women from her place at the front. "I have allowed my own intentions to interfere with our coven and brought death upon my daughter. There is nothing further I can say. I will take whatever punishment the coven sees fit," Violent said in the most defeated voice I had ever heard.

"We have witnessed the consequences of what happens when we lose faith in our coven and put greed above the well-being of our sisters. Violet Nary has been stripped of her title as an elder, but it is up to us as a coven to decide her fate. What say you, sisters? Shall Violet Nary be banished from Whispering Creek coven, never to step foot on our sacred ground again, and sever all ties with those within it?"

I held my breath. What Violet did was wrong, but she did not deserve banishment. Furthermore, Meadow and her sisters, even my Gran, did not deserve to lose her from our family. If she were banished, none of us could speak to her again. We would have to treat her as if she, too, were dead to us.

"All those in favor?"

I was shocked by the number of 'aye's' echoing through the room. We were a peaceful coven. We do not wish harm on others. Did they not see that this would harm her? She would be left penniless in a world unfamiliar to her.

"All those opposed?"

I, along with Meadow at my side, cast our vote against her banishment, but even as we spoke, we could hear that our wish would not succeed. Though many opposed, many more were in favor, fueled by their fear and turmoil of the events that had transpired. I could feel Forest squeeze my hand in support, but I could not look away from the scene before me.

"So it shall be, Violet Nary, you are hereby banished from the Whispering Creek Coven. You shall not step foot upon our lands or speak to our sisters from this day forth."

The other elders stood, raising their hands. I could see tears spilling down my Gran's face. Together, they began to chant, severing Violet's ties to our coven.

"Selene, ar màthair. Chan e Violet ar piuthar tuilleadh. Thoir air falbh i bhon cheangal againn riut. Coisichidh i a slighe leis fhèin bhon latha seo a-mach."

I had never seen this incantation performed, but we had

always been taught about it. The last time it had happened was when my mother was a child, and a girl from the Waldrick family cast a potent love spell on a married man in town after she had come to like him and hoped to make him fall in love with her and run off together. It was discovered after he came to the coven looking for her. The elders at the time could sense the spell on him. They removed the enchantment and then banished her. Without our coven, our powers weaken significantly. We can still cast, but it will never have the full force it would with the coven's power behind you.

When the elder's voices faded, Violet dropped to her knees. Her connection to the coven was gone.

"Your belongings have been packed, and you will be escorted to town," Pearl told her softly.

I could see that this was hard on everyone. Violet had been a pillar in our community and our unofficial leader for years. I held Meadow's hand tightly as we watched Violet led back down the aisle. I could feel Meadow pull on my hand as she started to go to her grandma, but I held her still. Once a witch was banished, we were prohibited from speaking to them. If Meadow went to her now, she could be punished as well.

After Pearl released the meeting, Meadow turned to me and cried into my shoulder. I held her tightly, wishing that I could take away all the pain and hardship she had endured. Her sisters came over and took her with them as they left. I went to check on Gran, whose cheeks were stained from tears.

"Gran, I am so sorry about Violet."

"That crazy old sister of mine. I don't understand why she was banished. She never intended to hurt anyone. Her grief alone of losing her daughter is punishment enough."

I pulled her into me to console her. I couldn't have agreed more. The fact that her crime was unintended should have been enough to grant her leniency against banishment, but fear is a powerful influence when tough decisions are to be made. With the death of Heather, one of our coven sisters, fear had struck at the heart of our community.

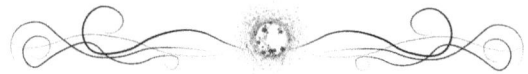

29

Juniper

F orest loaded our bag into the trunk of his SUV as I said my farewells to my Gran and the other women who had come to see us off. My heart ached at the lack of Meadow's presence, but I knew she was dealing with a lot right now. I had been hesitant to leave her at a time like this, but we had to get back. Forest opened my door, and I began to climb in when I heard my name called from afar. I looked up the trail to see Meadow racing down towards me. I jumped out and ran up to her, wrapping my arms around her.

"I didn't think I would get to say goodbye," I told her.

"Take me with you," she blurted out.

"What?" I asked, shocked at her request.

"Take me with you, please," she looked at me with pleading eyes.

"I-I can't. Not without the elder's approval. I wish I could."

"If they say yes, would you take me with you?"

"Of course."

"Then let me ask them before you leave," she nearly shouted.

"Alright," I looked over at Forest, who shrugged.

Meadow looked at Gran, "Will you help me gather the rest of the elders, please?"

"Yes," she smiled back at her.

I watched Meadow's long, wavy blonde hair fly behind her as she rushed back up the trail. Forest closed the car door and took my hand as we followed her.

"I should have asked you first. Would it be alright if Meadow stayed with us for a little while?"

He laughed, "Of course. She's your family."

"Thank you," I said honestly.

I was surprised at how quickly Meadow gathered the coven in the hall. Usually, it took an hour or so to get everyone together, but she had managed it in half the time. For her to go with us, she would need approval from the coven. Forest and I stood at the back of the room, watching everyone take their seats. Pearl, now the leading elder, stood from the table.

"Thank you for gathering so quickly, sisters. Meadow Nary has requested an immediate audience with the coven. Meadow, please step forward and tell us what is so urgent."

Meadow rose from her front-row seat and quickly made her way to the front of the elders. Clearing her throat, she stood confidently before them, "I would like to stay at the West Moon Pack."

The gossiping crowd's whispers spread like wildfire. Pearl and the other elders, all except my Gran, who had been at the car when Meadow first made the request, looked shocked. Pearl raised her hand to quiet the room.

"While we allow Juniper to live at the West Moon Pack,

she has a mate destined by Selene that allows it. We will not allow our coven to stay away from our lands."

"I do not wish to leave permanently, but I ask for some time to heal. In the last few months, I have lost my mother, my grandmother, and my home. My heart is breaking every time I walk through our settlement. All I am asking for is a month or two."

"And what of your sisters? They, too, share your losses."

Wren stood from her seat, her heavily swollen belly prominent, "My babe is due any day now. While I share in my sister's grief, I do not wish to leave our lands but grant her my approval to do so."

Willow stood next, "I wish to stay here to support Wren through the birth of her child. While I would miss my sister, I feel she is in greater need of healing. She has my blessing if she must leave us to find her peace."

"Juniper," Pearl called across the room, "Would you and your pack be willing to take in Meadow for one month's time?"

"We would," I said in answer.

She nodded her head before she looked over the room. "What say you sisters? Shall we grant Meadow Nary approval to visit the West Moon Pack for one month, under the guidance of our sister Juniper, so that she may heal from her losses? All those agree?"

The sound of approvals echoed on the walls, giving me hope that Meadow would be allowed to come with us.

"All those opposed?"

A handful of calls from those opposing could be heard.

"Then so be it. Meadow, you are granted one month's time to stay with Juniper and her pack."

She turned and smiled her big smile at me for the first time since her mother had died. The meeting was adjourned and she rushed to the Nary house to pack a bag. We were on the road within the hour and made good time getting home. When we pulled into town and drove down the road, Meadow glued her face to the window as she took it all in.

"This has been where you have been living?" she asked with disbelief.

I giggled, "Yeah. I thought the same thing the first time I came here."

We pulled up in front of the pack house and climbed out of the car. I looked over at her and couldn't help but laugh again. I watched her mouth drop open as she took in the towering, elegant building. Forest grabbed our bags from the trunk and led us in. Meadow twirled around in the foyer, commenting on each detail she spotted. Oakley and August came out from the offices as we approached the stairs.

"Oakley, this is Meadow, my cousin," I introduced.

"Hey there," he said flirtatiously.

"Hands off, Beta, or I'll whoop your butt," I teased him.

He held his hands up mockingly, "Yes, Luna."

"You remember August," I gestured to him.

"Yeah, hey," she said.

"It's a pleasure to have you visit us." he returned.

He was always so formal. We walked up to the second floor, where our guest rooms were. I had considered putting her in one of the spare bedrooms in our apartment, but figured she would like to have her own space. Forest had called ahead to have her room prepared. I pushed open the door to her little apartment, one of the two we usually reserved for visiting alphas. She gawked at the lavish living room and small kitchen.

"Is this your place?" She asked.

"No, ours is upstairs. This is yours."

She turned slowly and looked at me with a hint of excitement and surprise. "This is mine?"

"Yeah. The kitchen should be stocked, but we also have a kitchen downstairs and a cook who will make anything you need. Your bedroom is through that door there," I pointed to the right. "If you need anything, you can ask anyone around. They can help you. Oakley and August both have apartments on this floor, and like I said before, we are just upstairs."

"Thanks," she said, half-paying attention as she walked through the space.

She saw the television, rushed over, grabbed the remote from the coffee table, and turned it on.

"We'll let you settle in, and I'll come grab you for dinner," I said over some soap opera she was watching.

The show broadcasting so entranced her that she didn't even look to say goodbye.

It was nice having Meadow around. Over the month she stayed with us, I showed her my favorite places in town, including the gardens. I told her that if she were able to visit in the summer, I would take her up to the lake, but without a wolf, the hike would have been too harsh in the middle of winter.

She took well to the town and was welcomed by everyone. Day by day, I watched as the light inside her grew brighter, and she was slowly letting her pain go. She made friends with several pack members and was thrilled when I took her shopping. Back at the settlement, it was a luxury we did not get very often, and instead made most of our clothing and jewelry.

I always knew her bubbly personality would thrive in such an environment. My biggest concern was whether she would willingly give it back up when it was time to go home, which came to fruition the day after the full moon landed. I went to her room to collect her, knocking on her door before walking in. She was sitting on the couch crying.

"What's wrong?" I asked her, though I was sure I knew what it was.

"I don't want to leave. Everything here is so much better," she sobbed.

"I love my pack, and I think it is a great home, but Meadow, you can't stay."

"Why? You would let me, wouldn't you?" she looked up at me through tear-filled eyes.

The look of despair and pleading weighed heavily on me.

"In a perfect world, I would. But you cannot. If you refuse to return, you will be banished from the coven."

"Maybe I don't want to be a part of it anymore. I want to live my life like this," she said, spreading her arms out. "People are happy; they have families with husbands."

"Mates..." I corrected under my breath.

"Whatever...mates. But they have love. That's what I want."

"Meadow," I sighed, "You have love for your sisters, and your niece was born three weeks ago. You know you want to go see her and me..."

My heart broke at having to include myself in this conversation, but just as she fought the loss of her grandmother, I was still a part of the coven, and I was unwilling to give it up.

I could not lose my Gran, my connection to my roots. If she were to leave, I would not be allowed to talk to her again, and I wouldn't be allowed to give her a home in our pack.

I looked at her intently, "Would you really be willing to give all of that up?"

A look of hurt spread over her face, "You would leave me too?"

"Meadow, I would have no choice, just like you don't have a choice to talk to your Grandma. I am still a part of the coven. If you're banished, I won't be able to talk to you anymore."

"What if we both leave? I could stay here. We can have our own mini coven, just you and me."

"Meadow, I can't." I looked down, discouraged.

"Of course not," she spat out. "Why would you want to give up your perfect life? You have everything...the coven, the pack, this town, your mate..."

"Meadow, please. I wish you could stay here, more than anything, but I'm unwilling to give up my Gran. And I know you don't want to give up your sisters."

"Whatever..." she said as she went to her room and tossed the rest of the clothes on her bed into her bag. She slung it over her shoulder and pushed past me towards the stairs.

She turned and looked at me, "Have one of your wolves drive me home. I can't be around you right now."

The moment the words left her mouth, I felt a crack in my heart. She turned and disappeared from my sight as I sunk down on the apartment's couch. I could hear Forest's heavy steps flying up the stairs as he found me.

"What happened?" he asked concerned.

I couldn't find the words to explain, so I just leaned into him as he sat beside me and cried.

THE PHONE RANG as I waited for someone to pick up. Finally, I heard a shuffling sound as someone answered my call.

"Hello?" My Gran's voice came through.

"Hey, Gran."

"Oh, Juniper, I'm glad to hear from you. How are you doing?"

"I'm alright," I said, unconvinced. In truth, I had still been feeling the sting of Meadow's departing words.

"I'm glad to hear that, honey."

"How are you?"

"Good, just busy now that I've taken on the elder role. It doesn't leave much time for my cooking."

I laughed, "You know someone else could help you out."

"Pish-posh. I won't let one of the ladies come in and turn my kitchen upside down."

Gran was always a little territorial over her kitchen.

"Is Meadow around?"

"She's over at Wren's house helping her with the baby. Coral is just the cutest little thing," she purred.

"I can't wait to meet her. How is she doing?"

"She's doing great. I swear I even saw her smile yesterday."

"I meant Meadow. How is she doing?"

My Gran sighed. "She's doing fine. I do think the trip up to your pack helped her get over everything; she just seems...distant. She's processing a lot right now. You know that better than anyone; it will take time. Have patience with her."

I told my Gran after Meadow left that she was mad at me because she wanted to stay longer, and I told her she had to go back. I left out the part where she wanted to leave the coven, not wanting her to get into trouble. I knew that it was a stretch to have allowed her to come up here in the first place. If they found out that she didn't want to go back at all, they would never allow her to return in the future.

"We are heading to my father's pack next month. It will be interesting to see where he lives." I said, shifting the conversation.

"Are you sure you want to go?" she asked hesitantly.

My Gran had always been resistant toward a relationship between him and me. No one in the coven knew who their fathers were, yet here I was again going against the grain.

"Yes, I already told you I want to get to know about the other side of me. Wouldn't you want to meet your father if you could?"

"Not a chance. I don't even want to remember your mother's father. That old slog of a man enjoyed far too many drinks before I enticed him up to his room."

"Gran! I don't want to hear that," I gaged.

"Don't act all innocent, Juniper. We're both women here."

I could only shake my head. When I hung up the phone, Forest came in and sat beside me on the sofa.

"Any news?" He asked.

"No...she is still sulking. Do you think she will get past it?"

"In time. I'm sure she needs to find what makes her happy at the settlement. You told me she was always working for her mom. She needs to find her own place now."

"I guess you're right..."

EPILOGUE

Juniper

I had never been so scared as when the plane took off from the ground. There was so much noise and shaking as we crossed half the country higher than a bird would fly. Why anyone thought that flying was a good idea was beyond me. When the wheels finally touched down in Durango, Colorado, I could not wait to rid myself of the confines I had been trapped in.

August and a few other warriors had traveled with Forest and me as we made our way to my father's pack. After several hours stuck in that death trap, they called an airplane; we loaded up into two SUVs we had rented and started driving north. I was awestruck by the beautiful mountains surrounding us. They were different from those at home. These were filled with dense pine trees but lacked the thick ferns and ground cover underneath. The rocks and cliffs that dotted the landscape gave them an impressive feel.

It was nearly a two-hour drive to reach the pack, having to travel onto smaller and smaller highways before giving way to rough dirt roads. A tall metal sign held up by two massive log posts stood over their drive. "SRR" was cut out from the metal with horseshoes on either side. It looked like a legit ranch. Two guys in flannel shirts and worn jeans with holes waved us down as we started on the gravel drive. Forest pulled to a stop. As soon as the window rolled down, I caught the distinct scent of shifters.

"How you all doing?" one of the men asked.

"We're from West Moon, here to see Alpha Caspian."

Sensing Forest's alpha presence, the man lowered his head. "Welcome, Alpha. You can head on down the road, take your second right, and it will lead you to the pack house. Alpha Caspian will meet you there."

Forest gave a short nod before rolling up his window and continuing down the road. We could see little houses and buildings scattered here and there, but the massive amount of cattle was the most noticeable feature. On either side of the road wired fencing held in a swarm of black cows. I hadn't realized their ranch was this large. We followed the directions that we had been given and pulled up in front of a large stone and wood building. Caspian and a petite brunette with rich chocolate eyes, whom I assumed was June, his mate, stood out front. Forest walked around the car, opening the door for me. Caspian's face filled with a smile.

"Juniper, I'm so glad you could make the journey," he turned to Forest, "Alpha Forest, we are honored to have you visit us. Thank you for bringing Juniper."

"Anything for her."

Caspian turned towards the woman, "Let me introduce you both to my mate, June."

"Luna June," Forest greeted.

"Hi, Luna June. It's nice to meet you," I said slightly awkwardly.

I swear if I hadn't been meeting my father's mate for the first time, I would not have been such a hot mess, but I wasn't sure how she would take meeting me.

She smiled and walked up to me, wrapping her arms around me. "Juniper, I am so happy to finally meet you."

I froze for a moment but quickly returned her hug. It was warm and motherly, like how I had imagined it would have been like to hug my mother. They led us into the house, which had a luxurious cabin in the woods feel to it. The rough slate stone floors paired with the wooden walls were warm and homey. A grand staircase sat directly in front of us, and on either side of the room were massive stone fireplaces that warmed the space.

"We will take you to your rooms, and then we can all sit down to talk," June smiled as she led us up to the second floor.

Our room was one of the first set of doors immediately to the right of the top of the stairs. The room was spacious, with large windows along two of the walls. A massive four-poster wooden bed sat against one wall with a fireplace and a small sofa on the other side. They left us to show the rest of our entourage to their rooms. I peeked into the two closed doors off to the left, finding a large bathroom with a copper freestanding tub in front of more windows and a door to a walk-in closet that could also be accessed from the bedroom.

"This will do," I joked, taking in the opulent setting.

If I had ever thought that West Moon was the only pack with such grandeur amenities, those ideas were wiped from my mind after taking in this space.

"Do you want to shower before we head down?" Forest

asked as I played with the switch, turning the fireplace on and off.

I turned to him, looking at him with a pleading look. "Yes, please. I feel gross after that plane ride."

He chuckled as he stepped into the bathroom. I could hear him turn on the shower and quickly entered to join him. We took slightly longer to get ready as I didn't think Forest knew how to shower without bending me over and having his way with me, not that I was complaining. We returned downstairs and found everyone gathered in a sitting room off to the left. There were trays of food sitting on a sideboard against a wall with tiny little plates and napkins.

"I'm sure you all are hungry, so we whipped up some snacks for you to enjoy before dinner," June chimed in.

"Thank you, Luna June," Forest replied.

We fixed ourselves two plates, but before we could sit down, Caspian invited us to his office next door. Luna June joined as the four of us settled in.

"I wanted to give us a moment of privacy to make our official greetings," Caspian noted as he pulled June into his side.

They looked utterly enamored with each other, which made me wonder if that was what Forest and I looked like, too.

"Thank you for having us. Is it still alright if I call you Caspian?" I asked.

"Of course, you are my daughter," he smiled warmly.

"And you can call me June or...mom if you want," she said excitedly.

I took a sharp breath in. I had never thought of calling anyone mom. It felt sacred to the woman who I had lost.

"If it's alright, I will stick to June. I just..."

"No need to explain yourself, Juniper. I take no offense," she said upbeat. "Our situation is quite unique. I have to say I was in complete shock when Caspian initially told me about you, but I am just happy to have a daughter now."

So many emotions flooded me. I was grateful for her acceptance yet overwhelmed by my new family and their roles. I had played around with what this would be like, but somehow, I never thought they would be more than this distant connection. Yet, here they were in front of me with open arms, welcoming me in. I needed to set my thoughts aside and process them later so that I did not seem like a total head case in front of them. Forest held my waist, giving me a slight squeeze of reassurance. I was sure he could feel the slurry of emotions pouring from me.

"I would like to invite our sons down in a little while to introduce them to you as well. We have not announced you to our pack yet. Only our sons, my Beta and lead warrior know. I had hoped to announce it while you are here."

I gulped slightly at the thought of standing in front of his pack as he announced his illegitimate daughter, but I suppose that if he was confident, then I should be, too.

"That sounds good," I could not get past the awkwardness pouring out of me.

"Wonderful! We are having a bonfire tonight to celebrate your visit. We will announce it then," June lit up as she spoke.

We sat around for a while, getting to know one another. June had an optimistic, bubbly personality that took me a little while to get used to, but once I came around, I became more comfortable with her. I think it was the situation in general that I had been hesitant about. There was a knock at the door before three new faces walked in.

"Juniper, I would like you to meet your brothers."

I looked them over and smiled at them as I stood up.

"Hi, it's nice to meet you," I greeted them.

"I'm Jasper," the tallest one said. He looked serious, yet still smiled.

"Oliver," the one next to him, who was only an inch shorter, said, nodding.

"I'm Cain," the third and smallest one said with a goofy smile. "I can't believe we have a sister!"

"You're telling me, I can't believe I have three brothers!" I joked back at him. "I'm Juniper, and this is my mate Alpha Forest."

They each nodded their heads downward. It was customary to nod to visiting alphas rather than bowing as one would to one's own alpha. It was a sign of respect rather than submission.

"It's nice to meet you all," Forest said behind me.

"So, is it true that you're a witch, too?" Cain blurted out.

I could feel Forest tense behind me.

"Um...yeah," I said hesitantly.

"That's so cool! I never met a witch before," Cain chirped.

Caspian shot him a glare, "Cain..."

"What?" he looked back at his father.

"I have informed our family of your heritage, but I was unsure if you wanted others to know."

"It would be best to keep it between us," Forest added quickly.

I looked at him quickly, trying to read his intent, but remembering my fears of how my pack would accept me reminded me that it might be for the best. I didn't want another crazy wolf like Sienna to get any ideas.

"So it will be," Caspian replied.

We all sat back down, and my brothers told me more

about themselves. Jasper was training to become the next Alpha, while Oliver and Cain would become his Beta and Gamma, respectively. I had wondered how it worked when there was more than one male heir to the alpha position. Oliver and Cain were still in school, so their training was mainly in the evenings and weekends. Jasper had his own role within the pack and often shadowed his father to learn the ins and outs of how to run the pack. I shared a little about my upbringing and my life at the West Moon Pack.

After a while, Forest and I decided to head to our room to prepare for tonight. I was thrilled with how well it had gone. It was relaxed and welcoming rather than awkward and uncomfortable.

FOREST and I walked out back of the pack house to the raging bonfire. I could feel all of the eyes watching us as we walked through the crowd.

Other shifters are always intrigued by visiting Alpha's and Luna's, Forest linked me.

August brought us two glasses of whiskey. I still had not come to enjoy drinking too often, but on a night like this, I decided to partake. It burned as it slid down my throat, and I fought from contorting my face in disgust. Most of the Silver Ridge pack gave us a wide berth, but I saw them talking to our warriors. This was my first time visiting another pack, and it was interesting to see the similarities and differences from our own.

Caspian stood near the fire and called attention to himself. The crowd quickly quieted around us. June came up behind us as he began talking.

"Come over here," she guided us to his side.

"Tonight, we are celebrating the visit of Alpha Forest and Luna Juniper of the West Moon Pack. There is more to their visit than normal. I have recently found out that on a trip during the rogue wars, I sired a child. Luna June and I welcome her with open arms, as I know each of you will as well. I want to introduce you all to my daughter, Luna Juniper."

AFTERWORD

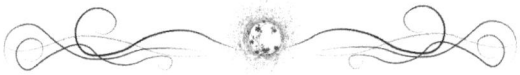

Thank you for investing your time in reading The Wiccan's Hunt. Your support, whether through sharing with friends and family or leaving a review on Amazon, is greatly appreciated. Authors like me rely on readers like you, and your actions can make a significant impact.

Thank you again. To read more of Ayla's books or learn more about her current projects, visit her website at www.aylavolk.com.

Until we meet again...

PREVIEW THE WICCAN'S CIRCLE

BOOK 3 IN THE WICCAN SAGA

Juniper

I gripped the worn leather reins tightly as excitement filled me. I glanced back at Forest, who looked far less thrilled with the idea of riding horses than I was.

"We have horses back home," I teased him.

"Yeah, but I leave them to Oliver and the others to handle."

I could hear Caspian chuckle as he lifted himself onto his saddle.

"We find it a better tactic to herd the cattle with horses. Since it is our main source of income, we all participate." He looked at me, "Make sure you don't hold those too tight. The horse will feel the tension."

I lessened my hold on the straps, eager to learn. We had been at my father's pack for a few days. Both he and June, his mate, had given us the grand tour of their land. Today, we were helping move some of their cattle up to another pasture. Besides the three of us, there were a handful of Silver Ridge men heading up with us.

"Alpha Forest and yourself will stay in the back with me. We will let the others take up the sides," Caspian told me.

"Sounds good," I smiled back at him.

He let out a sharp whistle, and everyone began moving. Snow still stuck to the shadows of the tree line, but the warmth of spring had melted it from the center of the greening meadows. It took Forest and me a few minutes to get used to riding, but the horses seemed to know what they were doing. We followed the herd of black cattle up a beautiful valley. A serpentining sapphire blue river flowed down the center, surrounded by a thick sea of emerald green grass that dissipated as the trees took over. The pine-covered mountains sloped upwards on either side of the valley, casting shadows on the glen below. It looked like a scene straight out of a movie. The beauty and perfection seemed as if only fiction could have created it, yet here we were. I took all of it in, savoring every moment of the experience.

After nearly two hours of riding, the sun began to take hold against the shadows as the trees opened up, revealing a thriving meadow. The first colors of spring wildflowers sprinkled the landscape as bees made themselves busy with their work collecting pollen for their hives, darting from one bloom to the next.

"Right up here," Caspian called out.

The Silver Ridge men whistled and ran their horses, directing the cattle across the shallow river into their fresh feeding grounds. I watched, mesmerized, as they moved them with ease.

"I wanted to show you two something while we were here," Caspian told us. "Let's go up this way."

He led us towards the hills, breaking back into the towering trees. A narrow dirt trail looped its way through. I listened to the birds singing overhead and closed my eyes as

I took a deep breath in. The air was crisp and fresh. I could smell the first of the flowers that had welcomed the warming weather.

"Where are we heading?" Forest asked him.

"You'll see when we get there," Caspian smiled back.

We started heading up the mountain through switchbacks that zigged and zagged up the slope. A part of me wished I could jump off of the horse so that I could be closer to the ground. I felt like I was missing so much from atop it.

"My father used to bring me up here all the time when I was a boy. It's my favorite spot on all of our land."

"I can't wait to see what it is," I told Caspian.

I could hear the crashing of water ahead of us. Caspian held up his hand, signaling that we should stop.

"We can unload here," he said as he dismounted from his steed.

He tied the horse to a branch nearby and walked back to hold onto mine as I followed suit. Forest dropped off his own horse and tied it up by the other two.

"Just a little further," Caspian pointed up the trail.

I was excited to be down on the trail with my own two feet as I took in my surroundings. With the strengthening sound of water, I picked up my pace, unable to hold myself back. We turned a corner, revealing a massive waterfall cascading down a rocky cliff face. A rippling pool of steel blue water sat at the bottom of the falls.

"It's beautiful," I gushed.

"I thought you might think so," Caspian smiled at me.

"Can I swim here?"

"It's probably pretty chilly. It's all snow melt."

"That won't be a problem for her," Forest told him as he watched me with amusement.

I started stripping off my clothes, nearly tripping on them as the eagerness took hold.

"Next time, give your old man a heads up," Caspian called over.

I looked back at him to see he had turned away. Forest stood beside him with his arms crossed over his chest, chuckling. I finished undressing and dove into the water. I could feel the strong flow of power pull into my body. I swam towards the crashing waters and dove underneath. It felt like an electrical charge revitalizing every inch of me. I came up on the back side of the falls and held myself tight to the smoothed granite rock face. I ran my hand up the stone, finding a good hold to steady myself as I bent my head backward, allowing the water to run through my hair. I could have stayed there all day, hidden away in a sanctuary amongst the water. When I turned around, I could see the shadows of Caspian and Forest coming to the pool's edge.

"Juniper," Caspian called out.

I could barely make out his voice past the thundering waters next to me. I dove back under and popped my head up on the other side.

"Juniper, I've been calling for you," Caspian worriedly expressed.

"I told you, she does that," Forest said from beside him, unfazed.

I smiled at him, "I'm sorry, I could barely hear you. I was on the other side of the falls."

I swam closer to the edge where they were standing.

"I take it you like water?" Caspian asked.

I leaned back into the natural pool, "I love it. It gives me energy."

"Her witch side," Forrest explained. "She absorbs the energy and power from the water."

Caspian ran his hand through his thick brown hair, "I guess that makes sense."

"It takes some getting used to. At home, I can't keep her away from the glacial lakes."

"I guess I chose right bringing you here."

"Oh, yes. This is truly amazing. I haven't had an opportunity to swim under such a powerful waterfall before. It's invigorating."

Caspian chuckled, "I'm glad you like it."

"You might want to settle in," Forest added, "I don't foresee Juniper getting out of there anytime soon."

Caspian nodded and took a seat on a rock outcropping nearby. I dove back under, swimming up the current. I stopped to look at the trout swimming by some nearby rocks. Their steady movements kept them in place against the water's pull. I enjoyed watching them and took note of their graceful, speckled colors.

It must have been nearly an hour before I made my way back to the side of the pool. Forest stood there with a blanket held out to wrap me in.

"You brought a blanket?" I asked, surprised.

"Caspian had one in his satchel."

"Never go without it," he hollered from the trees.

"Thank you," I called back to him.

I dried off and redressed, slightly disappointed to leave, but I didn't want the others to have to wait on me any longer. I could have spent the entire day there. As we rode back down the way we had come, I felt renewed and ready to take on the rest of the day. When we arrived back at the barn, several men came out and took our horses from us.

"June has lunch ready at the pack house if you both are hungry," Caspian offered.

"I'm starved. Thank you for taking us up with you," I smiled at him.

"Thank you for going along with me."

We joined the rest of the Silver Ridge Pack, along with our own warriors, as we ate a hearty lunch of chili and corn-bread. It was the perfect meal after the morning ride. The Silver Ridge Pack ate most of their meals together in a large dining room in the pack house. It was served cafeteria style, where everyone lined up at the kitchen window to receive their serving. Of course, the high-ranked wolves, including ourselves, were served at our table. We were sitting with Caspian and June.

"How was your ride this morning?" June inquired.

"It was amazing! Caspian took us up to the most beautiful waterfall," I told her.

"It is beautiful up there, isn't it? He took me there when we first mated. I never tire of it."

"I don't think you ever can," I smiled warmly at her.

"What's in store for the rest of the day?" Forest asked Caspian.

"I need to attend to some things in-house, but you and your pack are welcome to wander around and see what you can find."

"I'm heading into town to get some supplies if you want to join?" June added.

I looked over at Forest to see if he had a preference. He shrugged his shoulders at me, his go-to sign for letting me decide.

"We would love to join you, June. Thank you for the offer."

"Great! We can head out right after lunch."

Just as she promised, we loaded into her large suburban after lunch and started on our way. I decided to ride with June while Forest and August followed behind in their car.

"It's nice to have just us girls," she smiled at me as she drove off of pack lands.

"It is. Do you go into town often?" I asked her.

"Once or twice a week. It depends on how much everyone eats back at home. You know those men. They can put it away," she laughed.

"I never realized how much one being could eat until I joined the West Moon Pack."

"It's a give-away for our kind—hearty eaters," she smiled as she turned down a road.

"My boys don't like to join me too often. They always feel like their job is to be by their father's side, but as Lunas, we know that caring for the pack includes more than protection. Each person needs to be cared for from the bottom up."

I took in her wisdom, thinking of ways I could do better for my own pack. The drive was fairly quick, just short of half an hour to get to the town. Old painted wooden and brick buildings lined the main street with mountains on all sides. It was picturesque. We pulled into the parking lot of a small grocery store on the far end of town and unloaded. Forest parked in the spot next to us.

"You two are welcome to join or take a look around if you want. We won't be too long," June told them as they exited their vehicle.

"We will go take a walk in town and meet back up with you here in about twenty minutes," Forest replied.

I gave him a quick kiss before following June into the store. She pulled a cart out and passed it to me before pulling another for herself. I had only been to a grocery store once before when I still lived at the coven. I had gone with my Gran to get some ingredients that had been forgotten on our weekly grocery delivery. I looked across the ample space, taking in the aisles of the food and produce section around me. Bright fluorescents shined overhead, ensuring no corner was left in shadow.

"Do you shop for everything that the ranch uses?" I asked her.

"Some of the workers come themselves to get things, but since we feed them all in the main house, I do the bulk of the shopping. I have a standing order that I pick up once a week, but on days like today, I come to get some extras to tide us over until our normal pick-up day."

We walked towards the produce and started bagging apples, oranges, and a variety of other fruits and vegetables that they had in good stock. Before I knew it, June's whole cart was full.

"We get most of our produce from the store. Dry goods I get in bulk from the larger cities, and meat we cover at home," she explained.

We went down one of the aisles, and she began to fill my cart with juices and soda. We grabbed a few things down another couple of aisles before heading to the register.

"Good afternoon, Mrs. June," the cashier said as she rang us up.

"Hi there, Carol. How are your grandbabies doing?"

"Oh, you know how the little ones are. Busy as always."

"You're telling me. I miss when my boys were that young. Now they always have their own things to fill their time."

"Just wait until you have grandbabies of your own."

"I have a few years yet," she smiled back at the elderly woman.

We pushed our carts back to the cars and began loading the supplies into the back of her car. Once it had all been put away, we walked over to Main Street to look for Forest and August. Most of the buildings contained mom-and-pop shops or small restaurants. There was an old stone church near the center that I stopped to admire.

"This is an old mining town, so most of the buildings are from the late eighteen hundreds and early nineteen hundreds. A few have been rebuilt or fixed up over time, but they try and keep the same aesthetic. More younger couples have been moving in and trying to modernize the shops. They've added some clothing stores and even a 'chic' dog store," she informed me.

"What's a chic dog store?" I asked her with curiosity.

"It's all posh homemade dog treats and designer collars. They're cute, but I think they've set up in the wrong market. Most of the people around here with dogs are ranchers. No one is willing to spend that kind of money on their working dogs, though they do have some nice meat-covered bones, I suppose."

From my time living amongst the pack, I saw how shifters looked at pet stores. Watching dogs collared and leashed paraded around by humans could hit a raw nerve to some, though I still didn't have a problem with it. The dogs people owned were far different from what we turned into.

We found Forest and August walking out of a small store. Forest had a brown bag in his hand.

"Did you do a little shopping?" I asked him teasingly.

"I thought I would get you a souvenir from our trip."

He pulled out a long black dress made from soft cotton. The bottom had layers sewn together as they tapered down. It was in my 'hippy' style, as he called it.

"Thank you," I smiled at him as I looked it over. "It's beautiful."

We stopped at the little cafe and grabbed a drink before returning to the Silver Ridge Pack.

ABOUT THE AUTHOR

Ayla, a passionate reader and author of shifter and fantasy romance novels, is known for creating strong female leads. Her novels are not just stories but empowering journeys that delve into the strength women possess. Her character development is her strength, and readers will love getting to know them better and being able to invest their time into their tales.

Learn more about Ayla Volk and her books at
www.aylavolk.com

ALSO BY AYLA VOLK

The Stolen Heart

Warriors of the Eclipse

The Warrior's Calling (Book 1)

The Warrior's Bond (Book 2)

The Warrior's Proving (Book 3)

The Hunted (A Side Story)

The Wiccan Saga

The Wiccan's Alpha (Book 1)

The Wiccan's Hunt (Book 2)

The Wiccan's Circle (Book 3)